BLUE SUN

(A C. J. Cavanaugh Mystery)

Also by Michael R. Lane

<u>Mysteries</u>
The Gem Connection
The Butcher

<u>Fiction</u>
Emancipation
UFOs and God
The Family Stone

<u>Poetry</u>
A Drop of Midnight
Sandbox
Mortal Thoughts
Love & Sensuality

BLUE SUN

(A C. J. Cavanaugh Mystery)

Michael R. Lane

BARE BONES PRESS
P.O. Box 9653, Seattle, WA 98109

Published by Bare Bones Press, Seattle, Washington.

The characters and events in this book are fictitious. Any similarity to real persons, living or dead, is coincidental and not intended by the author.

Design: Bare Bones Press
Production: Bare Bones Press
Cover Art: Monika Younger

Bare Bones Press
P.O. Box 9653
Seattle, WA 98109

www.michaelrlane.com
www.barebonespress.com

Second Edition: September 2023

Dedication

Many thanks for the spiritual lightkeepers of my writing life.

Of all War, Peace is the final end.
                                    – Scottish Proverb

CHAPTER ONE

The two men had surprised Don Harriman. While he was behind a closed bedroom door working on his laptop, they slipped into his house through the back door. Don sensed more than heard them. He had hoped it would not come to this. Now it was too late. Someone had found him out and sicced the wolves on him. Until then he'd been both lucky and good. It would take an act of God to save him now.

Don closed the application he was working in and started a specially-designed scrubber program that would strip his hard disk of any activity. He yanked out the power cord and the laptop battery kicked in. Don waited for a couple of deep breaths, then tossed the laptop out of the second floor window. It shattered against the concrete walkway which he was aiming for. He hoped the scrubber program had enough time to remove any critical information beyond recovery, in case the laptop was not destroyed.

He clearly heard the intruders now. They were making their way toward the stairs. If the bedroom door had sported a lock, Don would have used it to buy more time. He raced to his nightstand and yanked open the top drawer. His Glock was gone. Don had been set up.

It was too late for the police. If these men were who he thought they were, Don would not live to hear the patrol car siren answering his 9-1-1. There was no way out. Circumstances forced his hand. He had no choice.

Don pulled out his smartphone to telephone the police when he saw a business card skewed in the corner, hiding away in the same drawer where his Glock should have been. It bore the name of someone he had been trying to get closer to, lately. He called the handwritten number on the back of the card. It went directly to voicemail. That took him by surprise. There was no time to try the office number printed on the front. He ended the call and sent a hasty text message to the same person; the sum total of which would become his brief legacy.

Two men wearing black ski masks burst into his bedroom just after Don had tossed his smartphone under the bed. Don rushed them. The second man sidestepped Don, leaving his partner to take the full brunt of his assault. Don was about to punch the man pinned beneath him when he felt something cold and hard pressed against the base of his skull.

"Move and you die," the man he had missed said in a bland, monotone voice. Don did not need to look to recognize the business end of a pistol; one that felt as though it were equipped with a silencer. He did not move. "Where's the diary?" the same voice said.

The man Don had tackled closed the bedroom windows and shut the curtains. Bright sunlight was reduced to back lighting, giving the room a sensuous feel. At gunpoint, they duct taped Don's wrists behind his back, and then taped his ankles together. Don Harriman could barely stand.

For the fifth time, the man Don had missed asked: "Where's the diary?" He was a tall man with icy blue eyes. His tone had mutated from stone cold to biting annoyance. He had yet to receive a satisfactory answer from Don. As punishment, he began to strike his captive, each preceding blow more ferocious than its predecessor. All body shots. Icy Blue was taking a page from boxing: Punish the body and the head will fall. Don could withstand the pain. For the moment, he welcomed it. It gave him something corporeal to grasp on to: life at its worst; but life nonetheless.

Blue Eyes' shorter, brown-eyed partner remained silent and nonchalant about the whole affair. He firmly held Don's bound wrists, now and then giving them a sharp, painful jerk. Don continued playing dumb. It was his only chance of survival. Blue Eyes hit him with a punch that knocked the wind out of him. The blow convinced Don to try a different response other than "What diary?" It might open a door he was currently blind to; maybe buy him time for a miracle.

"If you're talking about my real estate books," Don said, still trying to catch his breath, "I keep them on the computer in the den."

"Not those books—and you know it, asshole!" Blue Eyes snapped.

Don gulped, breathed heavily, then said, "Then I'm at a loss."

"We know you've been keeping tabs on the business," Blue Eyes said.

"I don't know what you're talking about." Don struggled to catch his breath.

Blue Eyes got in Don's face. The same mask openings that allowed his assailants to see and talk to him allowed Don a glimpse of who they were. Icy Blue had clear white skin, thin lips, dishwater blond facial hair, and matching eyebrows. Brown Eyes had dark brown eyebrows, white skin with brown freckles, fuller lips, no facial hair that he could see, and garlic breath. These were details that, Don knew, did him no good at the moment.

"Maybe this will refresh your memory," Icy Blue said, punching Don twice, hard in the midsection, forcing Don to double over. Brown Eyes let go of him and Don fell face first onto the pristine downy carpet. Blue Eyes knelt on one knee, speaking directly into his ear.

"Maybe I'm not being specific enough," he said. "We know the information's not on the PC in the den. We know it's not on your laptop, or any flash drives, or disks, or any other kind of peripheral you have. That leaves that little black diary you keep writing things down in. Now, where is it?"

For Blue Eyes to know about the diary, one thing had to be true. Someone had told him. Don thought about it for a moment while trying to breathe. Only two people knew about the diary besides him. One of them was behind this. Don bet he knew which one.

"My diary," Don blurted out before wheezing for air. "Is filled" . . . wheeze . . . "with personal stuff" . . . wheeze . . . "Nothing you'd be interested in!"

"Why don't you let me be the judge of that?" Blue Eyes said.

Don was not going to give them what they wanted. He suspected they had come to that realization as well. Anger and pride leaped in where patience and meekness should have prevailed. This game had gone on long enough.

"Go to hell!" Don said.

"You first," Blue Eyes said.

Icy Blue nodded to Brown Eyes. Brown Eyes drew his pistol. It was also equipped with a silencer. Brown Eyes pressed the weapon against Don's throbbing temple. Don was breathing a little easier now. An odd sense of relief washed over him as he accepted the inevitable.

"For the last time: where's the diary?" Icy Blue said. This was it. Don closed his eyes. He tried to pray, but his mind drew a blank.

"Oh, my God!"

It was a woman's voice. Don's eyes popped open. All three men stared at a woman in a crisp greenhouse cleaner's uniform, who stood frozen in the doorway. Her hands pressed to her mouth in disbelief.

"Run!" Don shouted.

Suzanne Kwong bolted. Icy Blue took after her in hot pursuit. Garlic Breath taped Don's mouth shut. There was the sound of two people running at breakneck speed, followed by a twinkling of quiet indented by the vicious slamming of the front door.

Icy Blue returned almost as fast as he'd left. Suzanne could be heard outside, screaming her lungs out for help.

"We've gotta get outta here," were the inaugural words Brown Eyes spoke. "The neighbors will be all over this place in no time. Not to mention the cops."

For the first time, Don saw concern in Blue Eyes. *A miracle*, Don thought. *Scream, Suzy! Scream!*

CHAPTER TWO

Suzanne ran down the hedge-lined walkway to the sidewalk screaming, "Help! Somebody help!"

It was mid-afternoon on a Wednesday. Most affluent suburban Crystal Gardeners were away at work.

"What in the hell is going on?" a potbellied man with a blond ponytail said, rushing to Suzanne's side with a loaded .45 in his hand.

"*Two men...with guns...,*" Suzanne squeezed out through her panic, sounding as winded as if she had just completed a marathon. She warily glanced at the weapon.

"What's happening, Lock?" A brown-eyed woman with wavy hair and tanned skin jogged up to them, settling on the other side of Suzanne. Both towered over the diminutive maid.

"I don't know, Jan. I just got here," the potbellied man said.

"*They have...Don...*" Suzanne gasped for air. "*Men...with guns.*"

"*What?*" Lock said. "What are you talking about?"

Suzanne continued her fight for air while struggling to speak.

"Just calm down, dear," Jan said, "and tell us what you saw."

Suzanne took in a few asthmatic breaths. She was hyperventilating. The few neighbors who were at home trickled cautiously onto the scene.

"I saw...two men...*with guns*...holding Don...hostage." The small crowd gasped.

"Where?" Jan asked.

"Upstairs...I think...they're going...*to kill him.*"

The crowd broke out into a worried murmur.

"I'm going in," Lock said, marching toward the house.

"No!" Suzanne said. "Didn't you...hear...what I said? *They have guns.*"

"What do you think this is?" Lock said, holding up his .45. "I didn't hear any gunshots. Did any of you?" he asked the crowd.

The consensus was no.

"In this neighborhood, a gunshot would sound like a canon being fired. That could mean Don's still alive. All I know is: we're not going to find out by standing around out here." Lock turned and marched toward the house.

"Wait!" Janice said. "I'm going with you. Don is my friend, too."

"I'm calling the police," a plump, elderly woman wearing Mom jeans and an embroidered tunic said as Lock and Jan entered the house. She separated herself from the crowd and made the call from her smartphone. The crowd huddled around Suzanne. Her breathing remained rapid, but she felt her hyperventilation subsiding. She continued to explain, as best she could, what she had just witnessed inside the Harriman house. The captive audience offered their ears, along with sympathetic words and appeasing looks.

"The police are on their way," the caller said a minute later, joining the others. Silence fell upon them. It seemed as though they were holding their collective breaths.

Everyone stared at the Harriman house as if it were haunted. The two were inside for a few heart-stopping minutes. For the people anxiously waiting outside it seemed much longer. When Janice and John emerged, they said they'd found nothing no men, no body, and no sign of a struggle. Suzanne remained persistent about what she had seen. The consoling neighbors had no reason to doubt her. The police were far more skeptical.

CHAPTER THREE

The weather was unusually clear and warm for early spring in Portland, Oregon. Local meteorologists were predicting a dry, hot summer. That suited me fine. I love hot weather. Love the sun. A sun worshiper in this part of the world is an oxymoron—or, perhaps, just a moron; depending on your point of view. But there is an intoxicating allure about the wet Pacific Northwest that keeps me here.

Perhaps the answer lies in the fresh air and clean water. Perhaps it's the rich diversity of deserts and mountains, lakes and valleys, rivers, beaches, and forests. Maybe it's the genuine respect Northwesterners show for the environment. Maybe it's the coalescence of nature, community, business, and art. Or just maybe it was days like the jewel I was experiencing that made bearing the months of gray climate worthwhile? Whatever it was, it had me hooked, for the time being.

I had crossed my six-foot-four-inch-long legs and eased my muscular body back against the firm wooden slats of a Waterfront Park bench. My deep green trench coat settled on me like a cocoon. My beige wool slacks gave my body room to breathe in the way that I liked. My investigative partner said my earth-brown turtleneck brought out the copper color of my skin. The same woman described me as her square-jawed, dimpled-cheeked, big handed, big feet, goatee-wearing, full-lipped, browned-eyed, razor-sharp, Coppertone sugar bear. She was wrong about me being her sugar bear in any way. I took her word on the rest.

Before me lay the peaceful Willamette River. Behind me, a wide stretch of manicured emerald grass flowed in both directions. To my left and right, apple and cherry blossom trees lined an equal stretch of paved walkway. Serenity rested her soothing hand upon my psyche, bidding me respite. I surrendered. All around me, people stricken with spring fever were at play at the feet of nature: a touch of Eden; a smidgen of heaven. I felt it, drawn for the moment into quiet bliss.

I had recently wrapped up a routine investigation for Lunsford Insurance. A policyholder had filed a long-term disability claim on a severe back injury he had suffered while on the job. I shadowed him for two months. Everything checked out. The man was recuperating, but his back injury was legitimate. I would recommend that Lunsford continue to honor his claim. That left one case on my docket: a suspicious house fire involving an even more suspicious burn patient.

The air moved delicately. All over the city, fauna and flora burst to life. The artificial ring tone of "The Razor Rim" by Wynton Marsalis interrupted my internal retreat for the second time in less than a minute. Only Destini and Renita had my cell number. They were two people in my life I dared not ignore.

Snatching my smartphone from the nylon holster clipped to my black leather belt, I checked my voicemail only to find the call had been terminated. A text message had come in. An indecipherable message popped up on my screen. The message made no sense. *Electronic gibberish*, I thought. Turning off the phone, I jammed it back into its holster. I tried returning to my serene state of mind. The mood was gone.

Renita had coerced me into having a smartphone. We already had home, office, and car phones that included voicemail systems, along with email, video, and digital document capabilities. We didn't need another line of communication as far as I was concerned—but not according to my tech-savvy partner.

"A smartphone is a 21st century necessity," Renita told me. "In today's world, you need to have instant access, so stop being a dinosaur."

"Nonsense," I replied. "Today's world was in little more need of instant communication than yesterday's. People have been suckered into believing that nonsense."

Renita didn't give up. She stayed on my case about getting a smartphone. Renita tried selling me on the ideas that it was a great way to stay connected to the office and was an invaluable tool to have in case of emergencies. I refused. While I loved being an investigator, that didn't mean I wanted it to inhabit every facet of my life. In terms of the emergency angle, Renita had me there. I could see how a handheld mobile communication device could come in handy in a pinch.

The world had gone into overkill with instant communication, as far as I was concerned. It had already redefined personal space. There was little opportunity for a still moment to pause and think. Every incident in one's life had somehow become worthy of calling, texting, recording or video recording, posting, or tweeting about. I wondered how much progress the great minds of the world would have made if someone were phoning, texting, or tweeting them every minute about some trivial matter that could wait for another time. Peace of mind was out of the question. It made me wonder if John Lennon's chant for an end to war could be extended to satellite communication, as well.

Renita didn't listen. My willful partner got me a smartphone. Renita purchased it as a work tool, citing that it would make us more efficient. I still wasn't buying it. There was nothing wrong with our efficiency. In fact, we were already incredibly efficient. Renita left me little choice. She had signed a one-year service contract on behalf of the Cavanaugh Investigative Agency. I have a soft spot for the kid. If I didn't, I would have fired her for making such an unauthorized purchase. Renita knew how frugal I could be at times, and was banking on that to force my hand.

She was right. I wouldn't let company money go to waste. I agreed to carry the damn thing for a year. If I didn't like it, Renita agreed we wouldn't renew the contract and that would be the end of it.

Destini had yet to call me on my cell. I suspected it was her way of not lending support to one of Renita's ideas. That, and the fact she knew I often had the phone turned off. That led me to the logical assumption that the message was from Renita. I decided to check it out in case the garbled communication was important. It was time to get back to the office, anyway. I needed to finalize my back injury report. I started toward my downtown office; but not before taking one last look around, at Eden.

CHAPTER FOUR

I found Renita in her office playing chess on her tablet computer when I walked in. She wore a vivid Adwinasa kente wrap dress and head wrap, tomato-red bead earrings with matching necklace and anklet, and a kaleidoscopic glass bracelet. On her hands were various handmade bejeweled brass and gold rings, an American version of a West African ensemble. Renita kidded me about needing to express her roots, knowing how I felt about mine. The colors complimented her smooth latte skin. Her high cheekbones, full lips, tiny ears, arched eyebrows, and diminutive flat nose gave her a regal air. Her posture was perfect; comfortably erect. For a moment, I saw her as a princess, majestic and refined.

"Damn! I don't believe I did that!" Renita said.

So much for Her Royal Highness, I thought.

I hung up my coat in my office and slipped out of my shoes before sauntering next door to see Renita.

"You called?" I said.

"No, I didn't," Renita responded, not taking her eyes off her tablet. "What to do? What to do?" she asked herself about her next chess move. Renita's forces were decimated. Her king was being corralled.

"I received a text message that made no sense."

"What did it say?"

"It didn't say anything."

I showed Renita the message. Renita removed herself from the game long enough to consider it.

"U%nV*q9H4zb?"

"Could be a password or a code of some kind," Renita said. "Or it could just be a screwup." Renita returned her concentration to her game. "Kind of like getting a wrong number on your phone. Call him back and find out."

"I can't. The number's blocked. Do you have a way we can get in touch with our provider? I want someone to check this message. Find out where it came from and what it should have said."

"Email, text, twitter, Facebook, telephone...you name it."

"Email."

Renita paused her chess match and moved over to her PC. She pulled up her electronic address book, retrieved what I needed, and emailed it to me.

"You couldn't write it down?"

Renita looked at me as if I were speaking gibberish. "Sometimes I think you just walked in out of the Stone Age. Now you have it for as long as you want on your own computer. As an aside: all of our smartphone provider's information is on our network. I included that link in your email. You're welcome."

"Thank you."

Renita was mistaken about the Stone Age remark. I had nothing at all against modern technology. I simply wasn't impressed by it. To me, it has been and will always be simply a tool. Like a hammer serves its purpose. So does a computer or a laptop or a tablet or a smartphone or other variations on the same theme. It all depended on what you were in need of, at the time.

Renita returned to her chess match. She made one of only two moves that were available. It was useless. Her king would be captured in three moves or less no matter what she did.

"Anything new?" I asked.

"Nope. It's been pretty quiet around here. Any suggestions on what I can do to get out of this mess?" Renita jerked her head toward the tablet.

"Forfeit."

"Not an option. You should play this sometime. It'll help sharpen your game."

"I can see how well it's working for you," I said, not trying to mask my sarcasm.

"Afraid?" Renita turned her baby brown eyes on me.

"Hardly. I have sufficient flesh and blood opponents who are challenging enough. You're excluded from that group, of course."

Renita smirked. *"Please."*

Renita had never beaten me at chess. I doubted she ever would. I saw no reason to drive home that point. "I like a little spontaneous trash talking when I play," I said. "Can your program do that?"

"Excuses, excuses. How'd the Bakerston case pan out?"

"He's legit."

"Want me to finish your report?"

"You'd do anything to get out of that match."

"Only trying to help."

"No thanks, I have to add today's stakeout information to it, anyway. Why don't you take off? It's a beautiful day. You know these are worth gold around here."

"You don't have to tell me twice." In quick succession, Renita forfeited and exited the chess program, shut down her tablet and PC, gathered her belongings, and headed for the workout room to change clothes. I deposited myself in my office, turned on my PC, and stared out of my office window at the powder blue sky while my PC flickered to life. I was working on the final paragraph of the Bakerston file when Renita emerged, wearing a spandex outfit that accentuated every tight curve of her athletic body. Beneath her bike helmet, her thick black hair fell loose into gentle waves onto her firm shoulders. Her Peugeot racing bike was at her side. Her West African ensemble was stored away in her backpack—all except the tomato-red earrings that she still wore.

"I'm thinking about opening the hot tub," Renita said. "Care to join me?" Her smile was inviting; her voice laced with seduction.

"No thanks. I've got a woman and you've got a man."

"It was a perfectly innocent invitation, C. J.—one friend to another."

"Sounds good. Mind if I bring Destini?"

Renita frowned. So did her tone. "See you tomorrow." Renita headed for the door.

"Be careful going home," I shouted.

"Likewise," Renita said over her shoulder, closing the door softly behind her.

I could not help but grin. I enjoyed blindsiding my partner's advances in the same way a mischievous child enjoyed playing harmless pranks on a friend.

Toying with Renita had brought to mind Destini. Destini was coming by my place that evening. We had plans to dine out. Once I finished the back injury report, I would email it to Carl Wheaton at Lunsford Insurance. Tonight, I would surprise Destini with a home-cooked meal. Unlike my business, homicide never took a vacation. Destini always had a full caseload.

A little pampering was exactly what she needed now and then. I was the man who would deliver.

I emailed Carl my report and then left messages for Destini at work and home as well as on her smartphone. I wanted to make certain she did not go through the extra trouble of dressing for dinner. As I phrased it: "We will be dining at a place that accepts you as you are."

Ten minutes later and I was out the door—but not before I had taken a moment to email my smartphone service provider about the faulty text message I had received earlier that day.

CHAPTER FIVE

When I entered my three-bedroom, English cottage-styled home, Booker and Andrew were there to greet me. The twin Scottish terriers circled my steps, barking and leaping all of the way into the kitchen where I set down my armload of groceries and gave them the attention they craved. After a few minutes of petting, belly rubs, pet talk, and mutual affection, I ordered the twins outside so I could prepare for my date, admonishing them to stay clear of my garden; particularly the roses. The twins slipped through the pet door into the enclosed backyard.

Booker and Andrew had always been my full-time responsibility. My finches and tropical fish had not. The house cleaner and I shared the care for them. Since my investigative work had slowed to a crawl, I had more free time on my hands. I told the house cleaner to remove my finches and tropical fish from her to-do list, making it clear this was due to no fault of her own. I simply wanted to get more in the habit of tending to their needs.

I was pleased that I did. It had become a rewarding and enriching part of my life. The house cleaner seemed a bit put off when I gave her the news. She apparently had become attached to them, as evidenced by her occasional doting touches in the aquarium and birdcage.

After dismissing Booker and Andrew, I washed my hands before making the rounds. Up next were my Zebra finches. Toussaint, Coretta, Claude, and Truth sang cheerful hellos as they saw me approach their cage. I asked each about their day. A quick change of paper and a refill of water and food were required. Next came my tropical fish. Everything in the aquarium seemed in order. Having finished attending to their needs, I washed my hands again and began preparing dinner.

In no time at all, I'd filled my spacious kitchen with sights, sounds, and aromas only present during the preparation of a home-cooked meal. I love to cook. Preparing a meal is, for me, not only a relaxing experience, but an art form as well. Once a month I'd try out a new dish on Destini or Renita or a few close friends. Most dishes turned out well. Those that didn't I either learned from or dismissed from the catalog of recipes I kept on my home computer.

Chante Moore filled my home with her sultry melodies of romance. The Twins and I periodically checked on one another. I peeped out of the kitchen window to make certain they were behaving themselves. They occasionally ventured into the kitchen, more interested in what was cooking than me.

Dinner was ready and dessert was baking when I went to the basement to check on the Twins' needs. The sandbox was empty. That was what I called a self-made wooden sandbox filled with kitty litter I'd built to accommodate my twins for those days when the weather was not to their liking. The dry dog food and clean water dispensers—also built by yours truly—were working fine. Their bowls were full. I took the bowls upstairs to the kitchen, emptied and cleaned them, refilled them, and put the bowls back in place. That done, it was time for a shower. Before doing so, I was careful to make dinner inaccessible to my roguish twins.

***

Dessert was ready and so was I. I had changed into a pair of loose-fitting blue jeans, a light blue sweatshirt, and my bedroom slippers. Destini was not due to arrive for another half hour. This gave me a moment to myself.

Meditation had become a daily part of my routine. Before my morning run, I meditated. It sealed a spiritual vacancy that nothing else could transcend. For some reason, that tiny bit of sacred time brought me back to the basics of life. A deep breath could become a fulfilling experience. All and all, meditation helped me appreciate each day a little more than was otherwise considered normal in our rat race world.

I tried teaching Destini how to meditate. She showed neither the patience nor inclination to learn. Destini said church and prayer were enough for her. My attempts to persuade her that meditation is the highest form of prayer fell upon deaf ears.

Any room in my house would do for meditating, aside from the kitchen, bathrooms, and basement. Of late, I had been consciously alternating among my Scottish guest bedroom, my Iroquois bedroom, or my Kpelle living room and den. Being surrounded by the particulars of one's ancestry, I believed, allowed me to become more intimate with my inherited roots. More to the center, it felt right; like an empowering revelation manifesting out of my soul. My Iroquois blood called me the strongest, on that day.

I took the Lotus Pose on the floor of the Iroquois bedroom facing the open west window after limbering my body by doing a variety of yoga poses. The sun was slowly closing her red eyelid on the day. I closed my eyes, relaxed my body, and focused on a point between my eyebrows. In no time at all, I reached a serene state of consciousness.

I had been practicing meditation techniques off and on for over 20 years. It was first taught to me by a dear friend in the service. Having had few distractions during the day made it a breeze. What troubled me most was the mysterious text message I had received earlier. Something about that message kept pinging away at my mind.

CHAPTER SIX

The doorbell yanked me out of my cerebral state. The twins were lying on either side of me. They were first to answer the door. I followed moments later, feeling refreshed.

"Here I am," Destini announced, stepping inside. I closed the door behind her.

"Don't you look snazzy," I said.

"You asked for it, you got it."

Destini had taken my suggestion to heart, wearing an old pair of blue jeans and one of my (borrowed — without asking) Pittsburgh Steelers sweatshirts that fit her like a short baggy dress, running shoes, and a Portland Trailblazers baseball cap that she wore backwards. Aside from chestnut lipstick and nail polish, Destini was au naturel. Her thin black braids fell loose to the small of her long lean back. Her mocha skin was satiny smooth and her clear hazel eyes put the sweet in sugar.

"You still look good to me," I told her. That's what love does to a person: makes Cinderella out of a dressed-down homicide detective. Destini discarded her hat.

"You're a liar, but I love you anyway." Destini smiled. Her dimples were on full display. Catching wind of dinner, she added, "I'm famished." Detective Pendleton made her way toward the kitchen.

"Hello to you, too," I said. Destini returned to me, put her arms around my neck, and kissed me. Her full lips pressed hard to mine, giving me a French kiss. The chestnut lipstick tasted like its namesake. I caught a whiff of cherry blossoms. Not perfume; lotion—a scent that beckoned me to hold her forever in my arms.

"Hello, C. J." Her voice dripped with seduction. I was ready to put dinner on hold. "Now, what's for dinner, my love?" Destini made a beeline for the kitchen with my ecstatic twins hot on her heels. I trailed the pack, telling Destini: "You'll find out soon enough."

***

We had a simple meal of lean sirloin stroganoff served with Italian bread, Indonesian Rice salad, a vintage Chianti, and for dessert, homemade carrot cake. As was typical, part of our dinner conversation revolved around work. Destini had finalized two cases that day. One was open and shut. It took a few days to bring all the evidence to light, but it was clear who the murderer was.

The other was the culmination of eight months of intensive investigative work. A married couple's son drowned in an apparent boating accident during a fishing trip. Destini and her long-time police partner, Dave Liederman, weren't buying the father's story; especially since the boy's parents collected on a life insurance policy worth a quarter of a million dollars.

Every investigative avenue the detectives tried became a dead end. Destini and Dave had already gone over the family's computer with a fine-tooth comb. They did the same with the suspects' office computers. In both cases, they found nothing. Backup disks proved futile, as well. Destini could not let go. Destini had put in personal time on the case because she was so convinced the couple had committed murder.

While pouring through flash drives previously believed to be blank, Destini stumbled upon a few electronic files. One of the files was named "Boat." That file had not appeared on any of the PCs or backup disks. That fact pique Destini's curiosity. It turned out to be a blueprint of how the father had murdered his son.

Destini later learned that the boy's mother had accidentally used the flash drive to make quick copies of files that she needed for work, ignoring the existing file folders on the drive. She had unwittingly used a flash drive on which her husband had detailed their murder plan in the file "Boat"—a flash drive her husband believed he'd destroyed.

Destini and Dave checked every detail of the plan. All had proved to be true. Case closed.

I had started a fire in the fireplace before dessert. Destini and I made ourselves comfortable on the living room sofa after dessert, enjoying the fire and sipping Chianti.

"I was introduced to a possible case today," Destini said. "It's a strange one. A call came in from Crystal Gardens about an abduction and/or possible murder. Dave and I happened to be in the vicinity, so we checked it out."

"You don't have enough work—you have to drum up business now?"

"You know how it is. The first 48 hours of any homicide investigation is critical. The trail gets cold fast after that."

"What happened?" I said curious about the would-be case, but far more interested in Destini.

"A house cleaner reported she had come to work and witnessed two men holding her boss at gunpoint."

"Anything to it?"

"No body, no blood, no sign of a struggle. The uniforms looked around and found no evidence to support her claim, although they had no reason to doubt the house cleaner's account. If her employer doesn't show up in 72 hours, then we'll presume the worst and launch a full-blown investigation into his disappearance."

"Could be a kidnapping."

"That's what we're thinking for the moment. We can't move on this until it's official."

"Do you think the house cleaner's credible?"

"She didn't seem like a flake or a drug addict. None of the neighbors saw anything, so they couldn't confirm her story. There was something peculiar that we did find. Someone tossed a laptop out of the bedroom window. We could tell where it came from by the direction of the impact mark it left on the walk. The thing was obliterated when it hit the concrete. The house cleaner identified what was left of the laptop as belonging to her boss, Don Harriman, the alleged victim; although I don't have a clue as to how she could tell."

"He could have tossed it out of frustration over something it did that he didn't like. Some people are temperamental like that."

"Anything's possible."

"Really." I put down my glass of wine. "Do you think it's possible for you to forget about work for a while, detective, and focus on us?"

"That's doable, Mr. Cavanaugh."

Destini put down her glass of wine and slid her body close to mine. I put my arms around her in time for a kiss. One kiss led to another and then another until our bodies spoke a language all their own.

CHAPTER SEVEN

I was glued to the computer screen, reviewing an insurance report on a suspicious house fire I was about to investigate. The adjuster suspected arson. There were some questions on how. Carl Wheaton would have normally used his own people to do a follow-up on such a case. It seemed so open and shut, Carl saw no reason to stretch his in-house resources any thinner than he already had. My job was to discover the reason behind why the fire was set. There wasn't much to it. The fire department would do all of the sifting, sorting, grunt and analysis work. All I had to do was connect people to their findings. Compiling a list of suspects was my first priority. Where to begin was easy.

My telephone rang. "Cavanaugh Investigation Agency, C. J. Cavanaugh speaking, how may I help you?"

"Remember that strange case I was telling you about last night?" Destini said.

"What I remember most is what we did in the bedroom."

"Before that."

"I assume you're referring to the case involving the house cleaner and a possible abduction."

"Make the abduction a murder. A couple of uniforms discovered the body of one Donald Harriman at about 3:43 a.m."

"You didn't call to tell me this. What's up?"

"We found your business card."

"*Where?*"

"In the murder victim's bedroom—in his nightstand, to be more precise."

"So, lots of people have my business card."

"Did you know the deceased, Mr. Cavanaugh?"

"His name doesn't ring a bell."

"Thought I'd ask; with you, one never knows who or what's going to turn up."

"What's that supposed to mean?"

"I'm pulling your leg, Mr. ex-DEA. Do you have any idea how your business card ended up in the deceased's night stand?"

"Harriman put it there, I suppose."

"Brilliant! We deduced the same thing. I repeat, do you have any idea how the deceased came by one of your business cards?"

"Every corpse with my card doesn't mean I'm connected with them. People come in every day and get cards from me. Donald Harriman was probably another person who found out something he was better off not knowing."

"Whatever the unknown was, in his case, may have gotten him killed."

"Sounds like a doozy."

"Snazzy, doozy—what's with your vocabulary these days?"

"A brother can't throw a little Mayberry R.F.D. your way?"

"Not without whistling the theme song first. Getting back on track—you don't have an explanation for the business card?"

"None. Am I a suspect?"

"Only in principle. It's procedure. I have to check all leads for the record. You know the drill."

"That's too bad."

"How do you figure?"

"I would get to see more of you if I were a suspect."

"You've seen me up close and professional before. I would've thought you'd never want to go there again."

Destini was referring to what Renita and I called the "The Gem Connection" case. It was a very trying time for the three of us; one that nearly severed my relationship with Destini for good.

"I'm long over that," I said. "I hope you are, too."

"Very much so. I still do my job the same way."

"I'm all yours, officer."

"As much as I enjoy our intimate little chats, I have to go. There's a lot of leather going to be worn out on this one. I can feel it."

"Free tonight?" I asked, hoping for a repeat performance of the previous night.

"Let's keep it open. I'll hit you up on your cell later."

"I seem to recall your being against my getting a smartphone, Detective Pendleton."

"I may be having a change of heart." I grimaced at having lost her support on that issue.

"Don't worry, C. J., you'll get used to having that electronic leash. I have."

"I believe you said you had to go."

"Ring you later, honey." I could hear Destini laughing as she ended the call.

I'd barely disconnected when Renita walked into my office.

"What's up?" Renita asked.

"Murder. What else?"

CHAPTER EIGHT

Mr. Derek Knopp was injured in the house fire I was investigating. He had suffered third degree burns over his entire head and body. The extent of damage to his skin, nervous system, muscle tissue, and internal organs had yet to be determined. Drugs, a respirator, and willpower were all that kept Knopp from cashing in. He was also my number one arson suspect.

I stopped by the hospital to have a little chat with Derek Knopp about his rental home burning down. That wasn't possible, according to his doctor. Rather than write the trip off as a complete loss, I used the time to take pictures of the burn site for eventual inclusion in my final insurance report.

The two-story, functionally modern two-car garage dwelling was one of a number of identical homes all over the quaint suburban neighborhood. Cookie-cutter homes, they were called. One plan fits all; minimum investment for maximum profit. I disliked that trend. A home, in my opinion, should resonate with character, personality, and a sense of individuality; not simply function as a place to hang your hat. If the foundation had held, they could have easily slapped together another house like the one that had burned down, in a month or less. It was certainly efficient. Progress: that all depended on how you looked at it.

In the middle of my photo session, I noticed I wasn't alone. Someone was watching me from a blue Toyota Camry. The person was far enough away to spy, but not close enough to identify.

I pretended not to notice. I treated my curious onlooker like a rubbernecker passing by a car accident. He was probably someone from the neighborhood wondering who I was and why I was taking pictures. Just in case, I decided to take some clandestine snapshots. By angling some of my shots so that the car and its occupant appeared in the backdrop, the onlooker was never the wiser.

I had forgotten Renita's digital and had picked up a disposable camera on the way. My plan was to have the film shots digitized. That would make it easier to make copies and magnify the photos, if need be. From that, I could obtain a license plate number as well as a better look at who my spectator was. One thing I've learned from years of undercover and investigative work is: you can never be too careful. Why didn't I use my smartphone camera? Good question. Let's just say that old habits die hard. Or, more to the truth, I had forgotten that my phone had a camera.

The Camry left a few minutes before I did. I dropped off my disposable camera at a one-hour photo shop near my building. I swung by the Fire Marshall's office to see if he had anything more on the Knopp house fire. He wasn't in. I told his personal assistant to have him call me when he had a chance.

It was midafternoon on another lovely spring day in Portland. While hiking back to my office, I heard live jazz dance in the air. I followed the music to Pioneer Courthouse Square.

Smoky was on electric piano. Winston was on electric guitar. They had a young man and woman who I didn't recognize accompanying them on drums and bass. There was no doubt these musicians were professionals. I recognized the song they were playing. It was an original, dynamic composition called "Wayward Sons" from their collaboration CD entitled "Questions & Answers." You could see they had reached that magical vibe known as "finding your groove". Each was feeding off the other, taking the song to a new place and creating a unique musical experience. When they stopped, delighted hoots, hollers, and applause rang from the large, toe-tapping, head-bobbing crowd.

I had made my way to the front. The musicians smiled, thanked the crowd, and gave each other high-fives. The crowd showed their generosity by putting nothing but folding money in the large three-quarters-full Maxwell House can. On the coffee can was taped a peach-colored piece of construction paper. On the paper was written, "Donations for The Rescue Mission are greatly appreciated."

The Rescue Mission was a local place that fed, clothed, and sheltered the homeless. Smoky, Winston and I had done years of volunteer work for the Mission. Now and then, the two jazz greats did an impromptu gig for their favorite charity. I dropped in a twenty.

"Hey, living large, what's happening?" Winston said. Winston wore his usual deadpan expression and near-delirious stare.

"Same old, same old," I said. "Trying to get by."

"Right," Winston replied with a nod and a sly grin.

"How you doing, C. J.?" said the man with a neat white beard and trademark baseball cap.

"Staying out of trouble, Smoky; and yourself?"

Smoky jerked his head toward Winston. "He's the only trouble I've got."

"You wish you had my kind of trouble," Winston replied.

"Not hardly. Your kind of trouble requires medical attention, if you know what I mean?" Smoky winked at me.

"Don't even go there, Smoky. You know I don't mess with no tramps."

"What about Rhonda Nelson?"

"Ain't nothing wrong with Rhonda."

"She's fine, I'll give you that. But she's fooling around with Tony Trellis. And everybody knows Tony has the clap."

"Everybody don't know squat. And for your information—*Mr. Busybody*—Tony and Rhonda have never been more than acquaintances."

"Oh, she's acquainted with him, all right, Smoky. In ways you don't want to recognize."

"*Gentleman,*" I said. Both men glared at me for interrupting their little squabble. "Are you going to play or what?"

The crowd chimed in with a raucous, "Yeah!"

"You like our music, huh, C. J.?" Winston said. They both had sly grins on their faces.

"Since day one," I responded with a genuine smile.

"What would you like to hear?" Smoky asked.

"Goin' Way Blues," I said.

"A little Tyner, Clark and Foster," Smoky said, "coming right at cha." Smoky and Winston informed the drummer and bass player who kicked things off. Smoky and Winston glided into the opening measures of "Goin' Way Blues."

I stepped back into the crowd, listening with adoration at their ability to drop heaven between my ears. They moved seamlessly from "Goin' Way Blues" into a parcel of their original compositions; one of which was the dreamy, melodic piece "Questions & Answers." I stayed, listened, and enjoyed. I made it back to my office eventually, humming a little "Questions & Answers" all the way. When I arrived, nothing had happened. Nothing had changed. That would not be the case for some time to come.

CHAPTER NINE

"C. J., can I see you in your office?" Destini commanded more than requested. I hadn't seen Destini since our dinner date the other night. A two-piece navy blue pants suit, sensible black leather shoes, a pinstriped shirt, and full-length trench coat were what she wore. Typical office attire for Destini, although a sharp contrast from the previous night; just as Renita had returned from her brief foray into West African culture, donning skintight gunmetal blue leather pants and a light cotton turtleneck.

"In need of a little morning pick-me-up, detective?" Renita said in an effort to rile Destini.

"No; simply privacy, dear—as if that's any of your business. So why don't you run along and do whatever it is you do around here."

"I know who I'd like to be doing around here," Renita said under her breath. I heard Renita clearly. Fortunately, Destini did not.

"Pardon?" Destini said to Renita.

"I said: I'm a partner in this investigation firm, and privy to any and everything that goes on within it," Renita stated with attitude.

"Renita," I said before Destini could respond, "don't you have work to do?"

I stared directly into my investigative partner's eyes to let her know how serious I was about putting an end to any confrontation with Destini. Renita got the message. Whether she would heed it was another matter.

Renita had a smug expression; one that I interpreted as Renita contemplating her next move. A look, I hoped, that Destini missed the meaning behind. It was the only way their sparring match would not escalate.

"I'll be in my office if you need me, C. J." Renita had a coy smile.

"Thank you," I said. Renita disappeared inside her office, taking her sweet time getting there.

"That was easier than usual," Destini said with a satisfied grin.

"Right this way." I didn't want to puncture a momentary settlement by responding to Destini's comment. I pointed the way to my office with a stiff right arm, following Destini inside and closing the door. When I pulled out the chair opposite my own, Destini politely accepted, sat, and crossed her legs. She allowed me a moment to make myself comfortable.

"What can I do for you, detective?"

"Remember that murder case I spoke to you about yesterday?"

"Don Harriman, the man in Crystal Gardens; the one who inexplicably had my business card."

"He's the one."

Destini handed me a sealed Ziploc bag. I found it odd the card was not in an official police evidence bag, but thought better of pressing the issue. I nonchalantly looked at it and shrugged my shoulders. "It looks like one of hundreds of cards I've given out since I've opened shop."

"Check the back." I did.

"How did Harriman get my cell number?"

"Is that your handwriting?"

"Yes."

"Since your cell number is only about a month old, that tells me you've had recent contact with this man."

"Right you are, but I can't recall having ever met or spoken to a Don or Donald Harriman. Looks like you've dusted the card for prints."

"Yep. Only found yours and Harriman's."

"Good to know you trust me."

"Simply doing my job."

"I'm still in the dark about this man, detective."

"Then answer me this, if you can. Why was your cell number the last call made from Harriman's phone before he disappeared?"

I drew a blank. I genuinely had no clue, and I told Destini as much.

"I'll need the card back," Destini said, reaching out her hand. I reluctantly placed the evidence in her palm.

"I'm withholding it from the chain of evidence for the time being. Only you and I know this card exists."

"I appreciate that. Around what time was Harriman abducted?"

"Between one and one-thirty that afternoon. We know that because the call and the house cleaner pinned it down for us."

That could explain it, I thought. Destini must have read my mind.

"You've got something?"

"No, just mulling over when I might have met Harriman." I didn't want to pass along bogus information to Destini. Neither of us enjoyed having our time wasted. I needed to wait until I had something concrete. I would put a fire under my cellphone provider to get a move on it.

"In the meantime, you're a person of interest in this investigation until this matter can be cleared up." Destini held my incriminating card between her index and middle fingers. She nonchalantly waved the card before her face, playfully depositing it in her handkerchief pocket. "So don't leave town without notifying the investigating officer of your whereabouts."

Her countenance was stern but not unpleasant. I could read her mind. Destini was attempting to piecemeal together the events leading up to Don Harriman's murder. I leaned forward, intentionally lowering my voice to a seductive tone.

"I'll do the investigating officer one better. I'll take her with me wherever I go."

Destini walked around my desk and sat in my lap. She put her arms around me and planted one right on my lips. "Don't worry, sweetheart," Destini said in her sexy bedroom voice. "This is all part of the process. You know how it works."

Destini traced my lips with her forefinger as if exploring them for the first time. She kissed me again. I wondered if we needed to lock the door.

"That still doesn't put a cork in my curiosity, or my concern," I said after clearing my throat.

"Meaning?"

"This man, this stranger—in possibly his final hour—tried contacting me. Why?"

"I was hoping you could tell me."

"I don't know why, but I will."

"Sounds as though someone's interested in doing some real detective work."

Working with the Portland Police was nothing new for me. I'd worked on narcotics or narcotic-related cases due to my DEA background. As a DEA field operative, I encountered far too many homicides. I became proficient at homicide investigations through osmosis. I had yet to fully prove myself to Destini. Even after The Gem Connection case. To be honest, I could care less if I ever did. The only reason I wanted in on the Harriman investigation was, as I had said, to satisfy my curiosity of why a desperate stranger had placed his fate in my hands. That, and the fact that it would be nice to nail whoever had murdered him.

"Do you mind if I look into it?" I said. "I've got a light caseload. A murder investigation will help keep my skills sharp."

"All right, secret agent man, have at it. As long as you stay out of my way *and* keep me informed of everything you find that might be of interest."

"I can do that."

Destini took my face in her hands. "I mean it, C. J.: any and eve-*ry*-thing."

"No problem," I said, meaning it at the time but knowing from experience how things could change. With doubt in her eyes, Destini kissed me again. Her lovely face lingered very close to mine after the kiss.

"Okay, honey, I have to go. We'll talk later." Destini headed for my office door.

"That's later tonight, I hope, in person."

Destini stopped in her tracks.

"We'll see." Her wink told me she would try. "Want a copy of the preliminary report?" Destini asked. "Once I've written one, that is."

"Let me nose around first. See what I can come up with on my own."

"You want it cold."

"As the corpse. Speaking of which; how was Harriman killed?"

"Twenty-two through the back of the head."

"Professional."

"Looks that way. We'll know more after the autopsy."

"Where was he found?"

"On the banks of the Willamette, near Milwaukie."

"He was shot then dumped in the Willamette."

"I never said that."

"I was speculating."

"Deduction without all of the facts—you are getting rusty."

"Was he?" I asked.

"Was he what?"

"Shot somewhere else then dumped in the Willamette?"

"It appeared that way."

I stared away from Destini. My eyes were set on the framed print of Jacob Lawrence's "The Builders" that hung on my wall while my mind plotted an investigation strategy.

"Remember our deal."

"Huh," I said, needing a moment to comprehend what Destini was referring to. "Like I said," I smiled. "No problem."

CHAPTER TEN

"Mrs. Harriman?" I said. A woman of medium height wearing a thick pink cotton bathrobe and fuzzy house slippers stared blankly back. Her lean face was drawn. Her puffy brown eyes were fiery red amidst her pale white skin. Her dark brown hair was disheveled. Her round shoulders slumped forward. With manicured hands, she clutched a large white handkerchief to her bosom. It had been three days since the death of Don Harriman. The widow of Don Harriman appeared as though she hadn't slept a wink in all of that time. The first suspects in a murder investigation are always the people nearest the victim—the closer the relationship, the greater your suspicions.

"May I help you?" Her voice was guarded and shallow.

"Are you Mrs. Harriman?" I asked. She gave a deliberate nod. "My name is C. J. Cavanaugh. I was wondering if I might have a word with you."

"You're with the police?"

"Not directly."

"Which means what, exactly?"

"I lend a hand on some of their investigations from time to time."

"I didn't realize the police were in need of outside assistance."

"They aren't. It's more like an interest of mine. A hobby, if you will. I'm an investigator by trade."

"With the police?"

"No, ma'am. I run an agency of my own." I presented Mrs. Harriman with one of my business cards. She stared at the card as though half-dazed, then looked back at me.

"I see." It was a reflex response. Underlying meaning: she could care less.

"May I come in?"

"May I see some ID?"

I showed Mrs. Harriman my photo PI license. Mrs. Harriman looked it over.

"Why not," she said, stepping aside. I walked in. Mrs. Harriman eased shut the door behind me.

The house was chaste; one that would easily make the pages of an interior decorator magazine. While it was bright, warm, and sunny outside, the climate inside was dull, stuffy, and dreary. All of the windows were closed and the drapes were drawn shut. What grabbed my attention most was the dead silence. It was surreal. Not so much as the voice of a bird could be heard. It was a pristine tomb. For the time being, at least, it appeared that Mrs. Harriman was burying herself with her husband.

"Did Don hire you?" Mrs. Harriman asked.

"In a manner of speaking, he did request my help."

Mrs. Harriman looked me over as if there were something familiar about me that she couldn't quite put her finger on. After a pregnant pause, she said: "You can't be too careful these days." I agreed with a nod.

"Allow me to offer my condolences for your loss." I tried sounding sincere. Mrs. Harriman appeared to buy it. She thanked me. Her eyes teared. I was sorry I'd said anything. I had hoped that waiting a couple of days would make her strong enough for some brief questions. I was wrong.

"Maybe I should come back at another time," I said.

"No, stay. I'm all right. Your company will do me good. I've been cooped up in here since I identified the body. My personal assistant made all of the funeral arrangements—closed casket, of course. It's tomorrow, you know."

I nodded with a slight smile.

Mrs. Harriman realized her mistake. "Of course you wouldn't know. How silly of me. Would you like to have a seat?"

"Only if that would make you more comfortable."

"It would. I'm not too steady on my feet right now."

Mrs. Harriman led me to her living room sofa, sat, and then said, "Where are my manners? Can I offer you something to drink?"

"I'm fine, thank you. Please relax." She tried, with a heavy sigh.

"Mrs. Harriman—"

"Call me Alice."

"All right, Alice. Can you tell me in your own words what happened on the day your husband was abducted?"

"*Abducted?*"

"It's my understanding he was kidnapped before he was murdered."

"Oh, yes, that's true." The widow Harriman looked around as if she were in a strange place taking in unfamiliar surroundings before her gaze settled upon me once again. "Can you believe it? They came into our home and did this awful thing."

In the snap of a finger, Alice Harriman stepped out of the fog and became lucid. "Shouldn't you be writing this down?"

"I have a good memory." An excellent memory would have been more accurate a statement. Not bragging; just fact.

"You weren't here when it happened?" I asked a question that I already knew the answer to. I needed to determine if Alice Harriman had any peculiar nuances, and if and when she lied. A twitch, a stutter, a momentary cutting away of her eyes or chewing of her nails—even something as subtle as a strained pause. Any involuntary tweak that might give me insight into her defense mechanisms, was what I was after.

"No," Alice said. "I was showing an out-of-town client various properties in and around Portland all day. Suzy stumbled onto that awful scene."

"Suzy?"

"The house cleaner, Suzy Kwong—she works for a house cleaning service we use. I can get the number for you, if you'd like?"

"That would be very helpful."

Alice was gone but a minute. She handed me a plain white card with "Sparkling Palace Maid Service" printed in bold black letters across the top. The rest of the information on the card, including the name Suzanne Kwong, was dwarfed by comparison. I thanked Alice, depositing the card inside my wallet.

"I'm afraid Suzy won't be of much help," Alice said as if it were an afterthought. "She's still shaken by the whole ordeal."

"When was the last time you spoke to Ms. Kwong?"

"This morning. I called to see how she was doing."

"Did your husband have any enemies?"

"None I could imagine would be capable of murder."

"You're in the real estate business?"

"Real estate and construction, we both are—were—are..." Alice struggled to maintain her composure. "You'll have to forgive me. I'm still a little disoriented."

"It's okay. Take your time."

After a couple of deep breaths, Alice continued. "My husband and I were equal partners of Blue Sun Real Estate and Blue Sun Construction Services. Our real estate company owns and manages properties. BSCS does residential construction. We're the largest real estate company in the entire Pacific Northwest," she concluded with a weak smile.

"Why the name Blue Sun?"

"When I was a kid, that's what I called days when you couldn't see the sun because of the cloud cover."

"Makes sense, especially here in the northwest." Alice flashed a bashful smile. "Does sole ownership of Blue Sun now convert to you?"

"Yes."

"Who's your insurance policy holder, if you don't mind my asking?"

"That's a strange question."

"I'm a strange man." My feeble attempt at humor was met with deadpan silence. Alice answered after an uneasy moment.

"Lunsford."

"What about dissatisfied clients? Any of them capable of something like this?"

"Not that I'm aware of."

"Competitors."

"None I can think of."

"How long had you been married?" I asked as delicately as I could.

"Two and a half years," Alice said, as if unburdening herself from the strain of a heavy load. "We dated for a year before Don asked me to marry him."

The thought occurred to me that they were still on their honeymoon, in terms of marriage years. I needed to know more.

"Where did you meet your husband?"

"Seattle," Alice said with a spark of enthusiasm. "Don had recently moved there from Cincinnati. I lived in Seattle at the time. Saw this great-looking guy at Pike Place Market. Our eyes met. It was love at first sight."

Alice's memory brought a distant smile to her face. She lifted a framed photograph from the end table nearest her and showed it to me. Don Harriman held Alice in his arms in one of those stilted poses so often arranged by professional photographers. It was a picture of a happy couple. I smiled and nodded. Alice returned the photograph to the end table, face down. I gave her a moment with her memory before asking my next question.

"What do you know about your husband's past?"

"I can assure you there is—" Alice grimaced. She stressed the word "was," then continued: "...nothing in my husband's past that would merit taking his life. Those dregs robbed me of the man I love; and for what—a few lousy dollars. Maybe Don wouldn't cooperate. He could be rather bullheaded at times. Don had a temper. Something probably went wrong and they killed—" Alice gasped at the thought of her husband's murder. "I hope they rot in hell." Alice muffled her sobs behind a sodden handkerchief. I wanted to comfort her, but I knew from training and experience that would be the worst thing I could do and remain effective. So I waited for her anguish to subside.

"I'm sorry to have to ask these questions. They are necessary."

Alice sighed, and then nodded her understanding as she dabbed the tears from her eyes with her handkerchief. "I'm all for it if it will help find Don's killer."

"I assume you've already supplied the police with all of the information they requested."

"I've given them everything they've asked for."

"Then I won't trouble you any further."

Nothing Alice Harriman did or said during our interview indicated to me that she wasn't being completely forthcoming. I waited a moment before asking my next question; long enough to catch Alice off guard.

"May I have a look around?"

Alice stared at me. Her eyes were filled with tears. "Do you think you'll find something the police missed?" she asked with a trace of suspicion in her voice.

"No. I simply need to get the facts straight in my head. It helps if I can proceed with full knowledge of the crime scene. Where did Ms. Kwong happen upon the abduction in progress?"

"Our bedroom."

"The bedroom is this way?" I pointed up the stairs.

"Second door on your left."

"Thank you. I'll only be a few minutes."

Alice Harriman was on point, portraying a bereaved widow. If she had something to hide, she was doing a damn good job of masking it.

The bedroom atmosphere was the same as downstairs. I drew open the curtains. The place was spotless. I tried getting a feel for what had transpired on that fateful day. There wasn't a clue, from what I could see. I looked out of the windows.

There was a skid mark on the concrete pathway where the laptop must have landed. I presumed Don Harriman tossed it there. For his assailants to do so wouldn't make sense. If they had suspected the laptop contained anything incriminating about them, they would, in all likelihood, have taken it with them.

Under a canopy of trees and bushes, the path vanished from view, about twenty yards in either direction. I closed the curtains before taking one last look around. True to my word, a few minutes later I was back downstairs. Alice Harriman was waiting at the foot of the stairs.

"Did you find anything?" Her voice was filled with hope, but her eyes told a different story. Still wet with tears, they bore down on me like an interrogator on a prisoner of war.

"Afraid not. If you think of anything that might be important, give me a call. You have my card." Alice pulled my business card out of her robe pocket where she had put it. Her face lit with recognition.

"Wait a minute; now I remember you. You're *that* C. J. Cavanaugh. The one the police detective asked me about."

"One and the same."

"She showed me one of your business cards."

I assumed the 'she' Alice was referring to was Destini. "She asked me if Don or I knew you. I told her I never heard of you before. She said she found your card in our bedroom. What business did you have with my husband?"

"I'm afraid that's confidential." I was playing on the client privilege confidentiality thing, hoping it would fly.

"My husband is dead. Who the hell do you think you're protecting?"

"That edict still applies."

"What kind of game are you playing, Cavanaugh?"

I took a moment to assess Alice Harriman. Her bereavement had shifted to rage in a matter of seconds. Her shoulders bolted upright and her chest was puffed out. Sadness had turned to steely inquisition. A defiant woman had emerged from the ashes of grief—a woman ready to take on the challenge, that, in her mind, I represented. That only emphasized to me that her misery was genuine. I saw no reason to hold back.

"To tell you the truth, Alice—"

"Let's go back to Mrs. Harriman."

"Mrs. Harriman, the truth is: I was probably the last person your husband called before he was abducted."

"Why would Don call you at such a time?"

"That's what I'm here trying to find out."

"What did he say?"

"I didn't speak to him. He left me a text message."

"What did it say?"

"I can't remember." Something in my gut told me to lie. Alice Harriman was angry and hurt. She had every right to be. Yet, there was something that didn't add up. Until I could figure out Harriman's message, it was to remain off limits to his widow. "You have no idea why your husband called me?" I needed a little misdirection; just enough to get me out of the door.

"None. I've never heard of you until a couple of days ago. And now you come into my home under false pretenses."

"I didn't falsely represent myself, Mrs. Harriman."

"You said Don hired you."

"No, *you* said your husband hired me. I simply allowed your presumption credence."

"Semantics: it's the same thing, you bastard."

"I'll be leaving now." I made a beeline for the front door. Alice Harriman was hot on my heels.

"Straight to hell, you lying son-of-a-bitch!" she yelled into my ear.

"Thanks for your time, Mrs. Harriman. I'll let you know if I come up with anything on your husband's murder." I calmly slipped outside.

"Get out!" Mrs. Harriman yelled. "And don't you ever come back!"

Alice Harriman slammed her front door, a thundering clap that slapped me in the back. Little did I realize that I had stepped out of the frying pan and into the fire.

CHAPTER ELEVEN

My knuckles were tingling when I left Alice Harriman. That only happened when I had a sense of impending danger. It took only a moment to realize from where that danger would come.

Two men were waiting for me at my car. One was about six-six, muscle bound, long black hair, square face, and eyes as expressionless as marbles. The other was about six foot, a brunet with a round face, average build, and laughing eyes. Something told me they weren't members of the neighborhood welcome wagon.

The smaller man was sitting on the hood of my car. The bigger man stood tall with his arms relaxed at his side. Stopping a couple of steps away from them, I angled myself to favor the larger man. Taking him out would be my first priority. That would make the smaller man less of a nuisance.

"You want-ah get off my car?"

The smaller man sneered as he lifted himself down. "What business you got with Mrs. Harriman?"

I smiled. "None of yours."

His sneer vanished. His light eyes flickered with anger. The big man hadn't moved; hadn't changed expression.

"Any stranger near that house is our business, after what happened to Don," the little man said. "Ain't that right, Tadpole?"

I glanced over at the big man. He nodded, crossing his massive arms over his barrel chest and stepping within arm's reach. The smaller man got in my face. He had coffee breath and smelled of cigarettes. His teeth were yellowed and crooked. A few scars mapped his stubble face. Tadpole was clean-shaven. There were no marks on his face, although his nose was bent to one side as if it had been broken and never properly healed.

"Now, you going to tell us what business you got with Alice Harriman?" the little man said. "Or are we going to—"

"I know, I know," I interrupted, sounding as unaffected as I felt. "You and Tadpole, here..." I gave a quick tilt of my head in the direction of Tadpole, "...are going to beat the crap out of me. Or express kicking my ass using some other quaint colloquial euphemism."

"You got it," the little man said. His sneer was back. So was the glint in his eyes. He really was enjoying this.

"If you must know—I didn't catch your name," I said.

"I didn't throw it."

"Right. Anyway, I'm trying to help find Don Harriman's murderer." Once more, his sneer vanished. His eyes widened for the first time, showing concern.

"You a cop?" the little man asked.

"No."

"Then what the hell are you?"

"I'm a—" I shoved the smaller man out of my face, followed by a vicious side kick just below Tadpole's right kneecap. As Tadpole fell forward, I ripped an elbow across his head, catching him square on the temple. With the big man on the ground clutching his knee and head and moaning in pain, I stepped back away from a stiff right jab from the smaller man. He continued his assault with another right jab, followed with a left cross. I slipped the right jab, blocked the left cross, and popped him with a right cross. It landed square on his jaw. Two right jabs—a left cross, a right upper cut to the belly and a left hook to the nose—were the combinations I dropped him with. The smaller man was down, but not out. I kicked him in his ribs, rolled him over on his stomach, and pinned his hands behind his neck, pressing my knee between his shoulder blades. I took a quick look at the big man. He was still on the ground, dazed and hurt. I hadn't broken his leg, but it felt like I'd dislocated his knee. He would be down for a while.

I returned my attention to the smaller man. "All right, let's try this another way," I said, using my free hand to tap his face off the pavement. He whined about his nose and side hurting. I let him know it could get worse if he didn't cooperate. The whining stopped.

"What's your name?" I asked. After he realized he couldn't break my hold, he answered.

"Alan Slankard! Get off me!"

"You wouldn't be lying to me, now, would you, Al?"

I yanked his wallet from his back pocket. His driver's license confirmed he was telling the truth.

"And Tadpole's real name?"

"Larry. Larry Paulozzo," Al said. Since Slankard had told the truth about himself, there was no reason to doubt he wouldn't do the same regarding his comrade.

Alan had an inspirational outburst. "A lot of good it's going to do you, shit-head! When we get our hands on you—" Again, I tapped his face off the pavement.

"Let's stay focused, shall we?" I said. The love tap seemed to work. I proceeded.

"Why the rough stuff?"

"You ain't seen—" I yanked Alan's head back by his hair. "Okay! Okay!" Al said. I released his head. He rested his face opposite the side on which a purplish bruise blossomed on his cheek. "It was like I said. We're looking out for Mrs. Harriman."

"Why all of the concern about Alice Harriman?"

"We work for the Harrimans."

"As what; sales representatives?" My sarcasm only amused me.

"We do construction work. Man, I can't breathe!"

Al's bloody nose was clotting, forcing him to breathe through his mouth; add to that the pressure of my knee on his back, and I could see his point. I removed my knee from his back and sat on his hips.

"How's that?"

"Better."

"As you were saying."

"The Harrimans own Blue Sun Construction Services. BSCS does almost all the construction for Blue Sun Real Estate as well as some other developers."

"And..."

"Don Harriman wasn't only our boss; he was our friend. Me and some of the men got together and decided we'd take shifts keeping an eye on his widow. You know. Make sure those bastards didn't make a run at Alice, the way they did Don."

"You're doing a fine job. With you and Tadpole looking after Alice Harriman, those bastards don't stand a prayer. Any idea who the killers are?"

"If we knew, we wouldn't be wasting our time with you. Those assholes would be fish food in the Willamette by now."

I believed Alan Slankard. Or, more specifically, he believed himself. Al and Tadpole weren't the sharpest tacks in the box. While I had their attention, I felt compelled to inject a little reality into their good-intentioned behinds.

"A word of advice, gentlemen," I said. "If I were a killer, and you good Samaritans approached me in the manner that you did, you'd both be dead right now. Think about it."

"We can handle ourselves," Al snapped back.

I was banking on the fact that once their wounds and pride healed, they'd give my words some serious consideration. I released Al and apologized to Tadpole for taking out his leg. They were pissed, but they'd get over it. In the meantime, those wannabe thugs gave me something to chew on. A look at the Blue Sun Real Estate and Blue Sun Construction Services personnel files were in order. How I was going to pull that off with Alice Harriman still angry with me was going to be sticky. I'd find a way to get around it when the time came.

A few of the neighbors stepped outside to see what all the commotion was about. I wouldn't have been surprised if someone had called the police. By now, a number of them must have had second thoughts about the increasing violence in their once-quiet neighborhood. I left while the getting was good, leaving Al and Tadpole to spin their own version of recent history.

CHAPTER TWELVE

Alice Harriman had neglected to write Suzanne Kwong's home number on the card she'd given me. It was a safe assumption that she had it, since she'd mentioned she'd spoken to Ms. Kwong earlier. No matter; it was easy enough to obtain.

When I spoke with the staff manager of Sparkling Palace Maid Service from my car phone, Mavis Gutterson was polite and courteous. She was a middle-aged woman, I gathered from her personality and voice, who insisted I call her Mavis. I informed Mavis that I, Stuart Brennan, millionaire financier, was actively seeking a new house cleaner for my Southwest Hills residence, and that Ms. Kwong had come highly recommended by my dear friend, Alice Harriman. An effective fabrication that in all likelihood would not be discovered—if at all—until after I'd gotten what I needed. If Mavis recognized the name Alice Harriman, or was aware of her recent tragedy, she made no mention of it.

I persuaded Mavis that a personal interview with Ms. Kwong was in order before I could make a final decision, making Mavis aware that a phone interview was acceptable. That lessened any suspicion Mavis might have had of me being a crackpot. What harm could one do by phone? Following an impromptu statement citing how irregular it was to give out an employee's personal telephone number (no doubt her artful way of informing a prospective client how far she would go to be accommodating), Mavis gave me the number.

Ms. Kwong was understandably cautious, but cooperative. I explained who I was and my role as an investigator on the Don Harriman murder case. My explanation seemed to pacify her caution. Before I could ask, Suzanne Kwong invited me to pay her a visit.

Suzanne Kwong lived near my side of town in Northeast Portland. Her place was part of a two-story apartment complex called "The Devonshire."

When the door swung open, a woman of about four eleven, wearing loose-fitting blue jeans and an art deco T-shirt that hung on her like a sack dress, stood her ground firmly. All of her features were small: her body, her face, and her hands. She was what some would regard as skinny, but I would call 'petite'. A straight, jet-black ponytail dangled to her hips. The cut of her face was full and round. Her skin was firm, a faint shade of tan. She had a delicate mouth and a rounded nose. There were several ear piercings, but no earrings and no visible tattoos. Her fingernails were polished the same plum as the toenails of her bare feet. Aside from clear lip gloss that brought out the natural pink of her lips, I couldn't detect any makeup. Shimmering black pearls stared inquisitively at me. We must have been quite a sight: a diminutive young woman looking straight up at all six-four of me while I introduced myself. At ease with my credentials, Ms. Kwong invited me in.

Her one-bedroom apartment was cluttered with paintings, carvings, sculptures, compositions and sketches of her own making. There was no television. A wooden case clock stood in the far left corner of the living room. Two wooden bookshelves stood next to it, painted in a Cubist style, overflowing with books of various sizes, shapes, types, and hues. A portable radio/CD/cassette player surrounded by a disarray of CDs and cassettes rested near the far end of closed white vertical blinds covering the sliding glass doors. Up two steps and directly back, a bantam dining area across from the kitchen was naturally lit from the open drapes; as was what I could see of her bedroom. Clothing littered her sparse furnishings and the floor. Ms. Kwong apologized for the mess. She didn't say it was temporary. From the way she navigated her way through it, I gathered it was her normal living condition.

Ms. Kwong offered me something to drink. Gracefully, I declined. She cleared a space on her futon for me to sit. In front of me was a bronze and marble coffee table with pheasants balanced on balls forming the legs. Heaped atop the coffee table were laundered clothes. Suzanne Kwong swept aside the clothes, sitting cross-legged on top of the table. You had the sense this was her natural state: a young woman comfortable in the simplicity of her own skin.

"How can I help you, Mister...?" Suzanne glanced at the business card I had given her that she was still holding in her hand, "Cavanaugh?"

"You can call me C. J." I glanced around at the variety of her work. Cubism, Modernism, Surrealism, Realism, Impressionism, Naturalism, Romanticism, Expressionism, Post-Impressionism, Abstract, Pop Art,

Minimalism, Dada, Art Deco, Collage, Photo-Realism, and Postmodern were all represented, as well as some I didn't recognize. Clearly, Ms. Kwong enjoyed experimenting. In my humble opinion, most of what I saw showed promise. A couple of pieces I considered brilliant.

"C. J. it is," Ms. Kwong replied, trying to sound authoritative as she slipped the card into the right rear pocket of her jeans. "And you can call me Suzy."

Suzanne Kwong did not look like a Suzy to me. That was a child's name. I saw her as a young woman. "To be honest, I'd rather call you Suzanne. It seems more befitting."

Her smile was radiant; one that more than lit up her face but also illuminated her person.

"I appreciate that, C. J.," Suzanne said, still sharing her smile. "Most people automatically shorten my name to Suzy, so I beat them to it. To be honest, I don't care to be called Suzy."

That simple gesture put Suzanne at ease. There emerged an unbridled, infectious energy; the type of youthful enthusiasm you'd find in someone who had not yet been anesthetized by cynicism and who still embraced life, welcoming all of its challenges and gifts not in the wide-eyed sense of an innocent child, but as an open-minded adult.

As Suzanne unleashed a voluntary stream of unsolicited personal information, I thought of Renita. Suzanne somewhat reminded me of Renita, in that fashion. A closer comparison would have been my fourteen-year-old niece. When my niece, like Suzanne and like Renita, is comfortable with someone, they possess what I regard as a gift. They had an ability to put a total stranger at immediate ease, placing them in a comfort zone as if they were visiting with a close friend or endearing relative. I had to confess I took a paternal liking to Suzanne Kwong. I had to remind myself I was there on business, not for a friendly little chat.

Before I asked my first question, I learned that Suzanne was 23 years old. She hailed from San Jose, California, where her parents still lived. She was the third youngest of two brothers and a baby sister. She had wanted to be an artist since she could remember. She didn't have a boyfriend. Had no plans to settle down, like her parents wanted her to. She had earned her BA in Postmodern Art from Reed College and would be moving to New York in the fall to attend NYU for her graduate work in the same field. Suzanne began working part-time as a house cleaner in her sophomore year at Reed to earn extra money. She continued to do so after graduating because the pay was decent and the job allowed her flexible hours to exercise her passion. And the coffee table Suzanne sat on was her imitation of a bronze and marble Armand-Albert Rateau Art Deco piece she saw in Paris that she absolutely fell in love with.

"As I mentioned on the phone," I said, breaking in when I could, "I wanted to ask you a few questions about Don Harriman."

Suzanne's disposition changed from cheery to dismal. Her eyes dropped. The energy seemed to drain from her body. Once again, I questioned my timing.

"Maybe I should come back at another time. Or you can drop by my office when you're ready to talk." I stood to leave.

"Even God asks questions." Her tone was somber. Her statement took me by surprise. She sighed. "Please sit down." I did as Suzanne requested. "Ask away."

"About what time did you arrive at the Harriman's?"

"A little after one."

"Can you tell me what you remember about Harriman's kidnapping?"

Suzanne sighed again. "I walked into the house. I heard voices coming from the upstairs bedroom. One of them sounded like Don's. I went upstairs to see what was going on. When I got to the bedroom, there they were."

"The kidnappers."

"And Don, he was on the floor. One of the men had a gun pressed to his head. The men didn't see me at first. I could see they had Don bound so he couldn't move. His eyes were closed. I remember saying 'Oh my God.' Don opened his eyes and shouted at me to run. I got the hell out of there. The man who was watching the other man, who looked as though he were about to shoot Don, came after me. I made it outside, screaming and yelling for help. The neighbors came. Someone called the police. After that, all I remember is answering a barrage of questions." There was a brief pause. "Don saved my life."

I nodded. "Do you remember anything about the men who had Don?"

"The police already asked me these questions. I really don't want to go through this again." There was a twinge of agony in her voice. It showed in her eyes, as well.

"I understand, but sometimes, after a while, things come to the surface that didn't register at the time."

"This means a lot to you, doesn't it?" I was surprised by her question.

"Yes, it does."

"The men were wearing black ski masks—so I didn't see their faces—and blue jeans, denim jackets, black turtlenecks, work gloves, and what looked like tan leather work boots. The man who stayed with Don had brown eyes. The one who came after me had blue eyes."

"Do you remember anything else about them?"

"Like what?"

"Their height, race, weight, hair—any other telling details that might help."

"I was hauling ass. I didn't look back. I ran as fast as I could."

"Maybe something else slipped through before you started running."

"They were both white," Suzanne said, as if surprised by her own revelation.

"What makes you say that?"

"When Don yelled at me to run, there was an eerie moment, like we were frozen in time, before I took off and the man came after me. I could see the skin around their eyeholes. It was white."

"Do you remember anything else about that incident?"

"There was something that I thought was really weird. When a couple of the neighbors went into Don's house to investigate what I was talking about, they said they couldn't find anything."

"Like nothing ever happened."

"Exactly," Suzanne said. "Some of them probably thought I was a flake. I think that's what the cops thought, too."

"Do you use narcotics?"

"No way; life's my high, as corny as that might sound."

I believed her. Not because I saw no signs of narcotic use, but because Suzanne gave me a strong impression she did little that was not in her best interest.

"What did Alice Harriman want when she called earlier?" I asked.

"To find out how I was holding up; to let me know I was invited to the funeral. Stuff like that."

"Sounds like you got along well with the boss."

"We didn't get along in a bad or good way. I was surprised she even remembered my name, to tell you the truth. I hardly ever saw Alice Harriman. When I did, she rarely said more than hello."

I filed that information away, as juxtaposed to Alice Harriman's concerned phone call to Suzanne. "What was your relationship like with Don Harriman?"

"We were lovers," Suzanne blurted out. I couldn't mask my surprise. "*Pardon?*"

Suzanne stared evenly into my eyes, repeating what she had said. "We weren't really lovers," Suzanne went on to say. "I mean, you have to be in love to be lovers. We were more like recreational sex partners." Her elaboration gave me enough time to compose myself.

"For how long?"

"Only the last couple of months. Don kept pursuing me. At first, I said no way. After I broke it off with my knucklehead boyfriend, I thought, what the hell—a good-looking guy, great body. It's not like I hadn't thought about it. We arranged to meet at my place. The rest is history."

Her energy was mounting, rocketing her back to the person I'd originally met. Suzanne elaborated a bit more about their illicit relationship with all the conviction of telling a friend about her favorite cooking recipe. I had to admit I liked her nonchalant attitude. I enjoyed her candor even more.

"So you weren't in love with Don Harriman?"

"Not for a minute. I liked him all right, but that was that."

"Did Alice Harriman know about your affair?"

"If she did, she never let on to me about it. Did you find the diary?"

"What diary?" I said, startled by this new revelation.

"The one Don kept locked away in his desk in their study."

"This is the first I've heard of it."

"It's all in his diary, or so Don told me," Suzanne said. "Don said he chronicled our sexual liaisons in it. I thought that was pretty cool. A little risky; but that was Don for you."

"He was a risk-taker?"

"I got the feeling he kind of enjoyed living on the edge."

"Can you cite any specific examples?"

Suzanne bit her bottom lip as her face glowered in thought. "I'd have to answer that along sexual lines. He was into both straight and kinky stuff; a little S&M, a little bondage, along with a variety of unusual sexual positions. Some of which I had never heard of before Don showed them to me," Suzanne concluded with a playful smile.

"Did Mrs. Harriman mention the diary during your phone conversation?"

"No, she kept going on about what a great job I did with their house, and she hoped to have me back real soon."

"Did Mrs. Harriman know about the diary?"

Suzanne's smile vanished. "I doubt it. If Don did put our sexcapades in his diary, it would be crazy to let his wife know about it."

"What all went into it? The diary, I mean."

"According to Don, any and everything—personal stuff, feelings, thoughts, encounters. I never got the chance to read it, so I couldn't really say."

"What about business dealings? Did Don say anything about including those in his diary?"

"Boring; but I'd suppose Don might have considered that stuff worthy."

"What did Don's diary look like?"

"Cheap."

"Can you be more specific?"

"It was about the size of your average paperback novel. Black imitation leather cover, gold-colored, inlaid lettering that read 'DIARY' and a little skeleton key lock that folded over the top like a hasp on the side." Suzanne demonstrated how the lock folded over the diary. "I'm sure you can find them at any store that sells that tawdry sort of thing."

"How'd you come to know about his diary?"

"Don showed it to me. I think he was trying to impress me on how sensitive he was. He wasn't. I mean, he wasn't cruel, either. He just wasn't sensitive."

"When did you last see his diary?"

"About a couple of weeks ago, we were kissing in the study when Don remembered he'd forgotten to lock it away. He showed me the diary, holding it up like he was posing for a photo op with the damn thing, dropped it in the drawer, locked the drawer, and we picked up where we left off."

"You had sex in the study?"

"No." Suzanne answered as if my question were ridiculous. "We kissed in the study. We had sex in the guest bedroom."

"Did you love him?" I had to be certain her earlier remark was not the defensive response of a scorned or remorseful lover.

"No," Suzanne flatly said. Her answer was not only curt but also definitive. I paused to take in Suzanne. There were no indications she was lying, that I could read. I moved on.

"Which one of you broke it off?"

"I get it," Suzanne said, perking up as if she'd just deduced who the murderer was in a spy thriller. "The girlfriend wants more from her lover than sex. She wants a firm commitment. Leave your wife and be with me kind of stuff."

"You've got it."

"Sorry, we were still ongoing right until the end. I wasn't there to clean the house that day, C. J. In fact, it wasn't one of my scheduled cleaning days. We occasionally made out in one of the guest bedrooms. But mostly we did our thing here."

"I see." Her candor, while refreshing, was a bit disarming. All of my instincts, all of my training, was geared to expose deception. Suzanne's candor made it difficult to keep my instincts sharp. If she had anything to hide, I simply was not equipped to weed it out.

"Do you think Alice Harriman had something to do with Don's death?" Suzanne asked.

"Do you?"

"The woman's tough as nails, no doubt about that—piss her off and you'd have hell to pay. But the one thing I'm certain of is that she loved Don with all of her heart. I would be dead if she found out about us; not Don."

"Did you consider Alice Harriman at all while you were sleeping with her husband?"

"Guilt, yeah, a little; but only after Don and I had sex—never before or during. He's not the first married man I've slept with. Probably won't be the last. It's funny," Suzanne added as if as an afterthought. "I don't have a problem sleeping with a married man if I'm attracted to him. I figure life's short; why not grab what you can while you're here. But let that be my husband fooling around on me and I'd be ready to castrate the bastard and skewer the bitch. Isn't that odd?"

"Odd, no; selfish, yes." Suzanne dismissed my comment with a slight shrug of her shoulders as if to say "six of one, half dozen of another".

"Have you returned to the Harriman house for any reason since the kidnapping?"

"No way! I don't want to go near that place after what happened! In fact, I'm taking an unofficial leave of absence. You're a very good-looking man. Mind if I sketch you sometime?"

That question would have derailed my train of thought earlier in the interview. But I had come to expect anything out of the mouth of Suzanne Kwong.

"First of all, thank you for the compliment. And, ah, sure you can sketch me, no problem," I said, moving forward. "To your knowledge, has anyone from Sparkling Palace been to the Harriman's?"

"To clean their house you mean?" I nodded. Suzanne looked puzzled. "I couldn't say," she responded after a long moment of serious thought.

"So your staff manager was aware of what happened at the Harriman place?"

"*Absolutely.* I told Mavis myself, leaving out the part about why I was really there. I made her believe I'd received an emergency call from Mr. Harriman wanting me to help him set up for a special dinner he had planned for his wife. You won't bust me, will you?"

"No," I said, giving some thought to how the pieces of the Harriman case were starting to fit together.

"What about now?" Suzanne said, disturbing my train of thought.

"Now what?

"The sketch."

"Some other time. I've got to get going."

"It would only take a minute for me to grab my sketchpad."

"Next time." Suzanne was visibly disappointed. My paternal side kicked in. "I promise." Suzanne smiled. All was right with her world for the moment.

Our interview was over. Suzanne walked me to the door.

"I'm really sorry Don's dead," Suzanne said with sincere gravity. "Don was a good man. I'm not saying that because we were intimate. That's coming from my heart." Suzanne pointed to her heart. Tears flowed freely down her cheeks. Then the sobbing started. When she hugged me, I was disconcerted. I felt as though she were a child in need of comfort. I put my arms around her, holding her until her sobbing ceased.

"So when will I see you again?" Suzanne asked, wiping away her tears on the handkerchief I had handed her.

"Pardon?"

"To sketch you."

"Drop by the office when you have a chance. We'll do it then."

"I will."

"Are you going to be all right?" I asked.

"Yeah, as soon as I get the guilt and grief out of my system."

"You have my card. Call if you remember anything, or if you just want to talk."

"Thanks," Suzanne said before I left with a possible motive for murder.

CHAPTER THIRTEEN

I telephoned the staff manager of Sparkling Palace Maid Service on my drive back to the office.

"Suzanne is a lovely young woman," I said in a tone beaming with praise, "who for the moment I regard as my number one choice."

"I'm so glad you liked her, Mr. Brennan." Mavis sounded pleased. "Suzy is one of our best. Would you care to start scheduling her?" There was that dreaded "Suzy" Suzanne did not care for. I fought my impulse to correct Mavis Gutterson.

"Not yet; there is one other person I would like to interview."

"Who might that be?"

"The person who last cleaned Alice Harriman's home."

"That would have been Suzy."

"Are you certain?"

"I'm sorry. I don't follow, Mr. Brennan."

"On my last visit to Alice's—which was today, actually—her place was spotless. Suzy said she hadn't been there since the time of the tragedy. Did you hear about what happened to poor Don Harriman?"

"Yes, I did. It was on the news and in the newspapers. How could such a terrible thing have happened?" Her sentiments were sincere, although she wisely omitted her original source of information.

"Indeed," I said, not wanting to rush and awaken any suspicion.

"You were saying, Mr. Brennan, about Suzy."

"Oh, yes! Suzy said she had not cleaned Alice's place since before Don Harriman was kidnapped. I presumed someone else from your agency had done such a magnificent job of house cleaning."

"I don't think anyone else has been there since Suzy. Let me check."

There was a protracted pause. I could hear the clicking of computer keys. "My records don't show us dispatching anyone to the Harriman house."

"Are you certain?"

"Positive, sir."

"Oh, that's right. Alice did mention something about the neighbors pitching in during this stressful period in her life. Maybe they helped with the cleaning."

"That could be. Mrs. Harriman could certainly answer that for you."

She most certainly could, I thought. *All I need do is ask. Then that would alert Alice Harriman to my suspicions. That would never do.*

"With your approval, sir, we can get the paperwork going—"

"Before I make any commitments..." Knowing where Mavis was going with her last statement, I cut her off. "I'll need to discuss it with my better half. She'll be the one coordinating most of the housework. You do understand, don't you?"

"Of course, Mr. Brennan," Mavis said. Her voice was terse. *She'll get over it,* I thought. "Thanks for your time and assistance."

"Do keep us in mind." The congeniality in her voice had taken a sharp turn from sincere to forced.

"I certainly will. Again, thanks for all of your help."

"Any time, Mr. Brennan. Give my best to your wife."

"Will do."

When I hung up, I was clear about one thing. Don Harriman was not a haphazard kidnapping attempt gone awry. There were professionals involved; people knowledgeable in murder who were covering their tracks. Who and why? Answers to those two questions rolled over and over in my mind.

CHAPTER FOURTEEN

I persuaded Destini to have dinner with me despite her protest of a heavy caseload. Destini was in the mood for Italian. I chose a popular Italian restaurant on the wharf with an unobstructed view of the Willamette River: a place steeped in typical Italian American ambiance with piped in violins, red-checkered tablecloths, and inviting candlelight. One could have dubbed it a romantic setting. For me, the place was too well-lit, too vibrant, and too large to don that intimate label.

I expected Destini to arrive in her work clothes. When she approached me wearing high heels, a full complement of makeup, and a knee-length, spaghetti-strapped lavender dress that earned salacious male stares and envious female glares, I was taken aback. Her fine black braids were tied back from her beautiful oval face. With each confident stride, her hazel eyes beamed brighter and her mocha skin became more enticing.

"Good evening," Destini said with a soft, wet smile. I stared at Destini, speechless. There is a quaint expression that in part reads "a vision of loveliness". I witnessed those words manifest.

My priorities shifted. I had invited Destini to dinner to spend quality time with her. Discussing the Harriman case was secondary on my list. On seeing Destini, a revelation came over me. Romance was where you found it. Desire swelled in me for more than a goodnight kiss and thanks for a lovely dinner.

We hugged, kissed, and then I helped Destini with her chair. A light seductive fragrance of peach blossoms lingered with me as I returned to my seat.

"Sorry I'm late," Destini said. Her voice was both refined and vibrant.

"You're a vision that was worth the wait." My sincerity came through.

"Thank you." Her smile was appreciative; knowing that made me almost giddy. For a romantically experienced, sophisticated man, that was quite a feat.

"Mind if we order?" Destini said. "I'm famished."

We ordered our meals, then relaxed with a glass of red wine.

"Tell me what has you so busy these days?" I asked. I would have been content simply to stare at Destini for a while. Drink in her beauty. Sup on her delicious charm, nibble after succulent nibble. If we were alone, I would have made my feelings evident via the most sensual means of human interaction. Being in public required a more sociably acceptable approach.

Destini explained that she was more than pleased to have someone she could trust working on the Harriman case. Her caseload had unexpectedly tripled due to emergency medical leave by two of her colleagues. She informed me that she was going to handle the Harriman case as if she were delegating it to me. I promised to do my best. I also promised to keep my involvement in the case low-key. That way, when I wrapped up the case, I could hand it over to her and she could follow through without a hitch. Provided I managed to wrap it up.

Destini made it clear that for all intents and purposes, my being the principal in the Harriman case did not mean I had free range. I knew I would have to watch how I proceeded. All investigators are sensitive about other people—particularly other investigators—treading on their territory. Destini exhibited that quality in triplicate. As long as I kept my word, and kept her apprised, there would be no problems. Cross her and my life could become very interesting in a burning in hell sort of way.

"It's like I told you before: that's what you get for being good at your job," I said in reference to her heavy caseload, inferring the confidence that her chief had in her to be able to handle the additional work. Destini took my compliment in stride.

"Try 'great at my job' and I might believe you," she said.

"Great it is." We raised our wine glasses in toast to her greatness.

"What is it you wanted to discuss face-to-face, C. J.?" Her tone was sweet and seductively playful. I hated to do it, but it was necessary. I switched gears from pleasure to business.

"It's about the Harriman case."

"Oh!" Destini looked and sounded disappointed. "Is that it?"

I wondered if Destini were expecting something else. "I'm afraid so," I said, trying to pinpoint what was going on. Had I missed something? Had I done something to imply more than dinner? I racked my brain for the answer. Nothing came to mind. Destini's demeanor went from warm and inviting to stern and intense.

"I'm listening," she snapped.

Not knowing what else to do, I cleared my throat and began. "I know Don Harriman. At least, I've met him before."

"Spare me the drama and get to the details." Her tone was gruff. She sipped her wine. I continued pretending not to notice.

"I saw a photo of Harriman while interviewing the widow. We met on the night I stood in for Ernest to coach his midnight league basketball team. Harriman introduced himself to me as Barrette Wells, a local businessman interested in doing volunteer work at the community center. At the time he sounded so enthusiastic about wanting to help, I leaped at the possible support. We didn't have an opportunity to discuss how he planned to involve himself. He said he was late for an important meeting and would get back to me. What sort of meeting one would have after midnight, I didn't ask. I wrote my cell number on the back of one of my business cards and gave it to him. I didn't mention it was my cell number. I assumed he'd figure it out for himself. There was no way to know that he'd be dead shortly thereafter."

"When was this?"

"About a month before his death. I had crossed him off as all talk and no action."

"You met him at the center?" Destini took another sip of wine.

"Correct. There's more. The maid confirmed she witnessed his abduction a little after one that afternoon."

"We already know that."

"It was around that time I received a strange text message."

Destini's eyes narrowed. "You never told me about any message."

"I thought it was an error; a glitch in their system. When you mentioned the abduction time in my office, something clicked."

Destini's eyes reset to their beautiful norm. That told me she was satisfied with my explanation. "Go on," she said.

"I emailed my service providers—"

"If you thought it was unimportant, why'd you email your smartphone provider?" Destini asked. "Why didn't you just call them?"

"Are you going to allow me to finish?"

Destini sighed, then stared at me for a moment. She was sizing me up. Trying to determine what information I was leaving out of my answers. Her tone was snippy when she spoke. "Continue."

"In answer to your question, I'd hoped they could tell me what the message was supposed to say—and in hindsight, I would have called if I had it to do over again. Happy?"

"Ecstatic. Were they?"

"Were they what?"

"Able to tell you what the message said."

"It took them long enough, but when they finally got back to me, the message I queried them about checked out. It was sent as received. There was no mistake." I wrote down the message on my notepad, tore it out, and gave the slip of paper to Destini. "You may want to check it against Harriman's files, records—"

"I know the drill. Been there, done that."

"You already knew about the text message."

"Of course."

"Why didn't you say anything?"

"Why didn't you?" Destini waved her hand across her face as if to dismiss the question. "Since you're working full time on the case, and I'm swamped, I thought it better for you to pursue the lead undaunted by any previous results."

Destini sounded irritated. I could relate to how she felt. I wasn't giving her the whole story, and Destini sensed it. Now she was trying to determine how long of a leash to give me before reeling me in. If that's what was bothering her. If it were something of a more personal nature, there might not be a short-term recovery. I preferred not to think about that option.

"It looks like a password or serial code," Destini said, studying the information I handed her. "We couldn't figure out to what."

"We're at the same dead end, but there's one more thing." I paused to assure Destini's full attention. Destini had slipped into detective mode, absorbing every drop of information.

"Why didn't he call you at the office?" Destini said. She must have read my mind. I tried not to, but I couldn't help flashing a smile. My smile was not returned. I leaned forward. Destini did the same. Her eyes narrowed. I could tell the thrill of the hunt was taking hold. Whatever had her upset had taken a temporary back seat. I took a moment to relish her delicate peach blossom scent.

"My guess is Harriman thought he couldn't chance calling me at the office. He'd never been to my office. He couldn't be certain who or what to expect. The other number was a safer gamble."

"Go on."

"In his haste, Harriman dialed my cell number, mistaking it for my home number. His intent was to speak to me or leave a message. By the time he discovered it was my cell number, it was too late. He did what he could by passing along that message as his last will and testament."

"Anything else?"

"Not for now."

"Why did Harriman lie about his identity?" Destini asked.

"That's something you'll know as soon as I know."

"Any leads?"

"Just my gut."

"I see you have a cut on your right knuckle." There was an unexpected playfulness in her voice. I loved the way she held back certain observations, waiting for the right moment to spring them on me. It kept me on my toes. "Brought on by a little skirmish with anybody I should know about?"

"In time, my love, in time. I need those boneheads loose. They may lead to bigger fish."

"Let me make one thing perfectly clear," Destini said, with all the power of a dignified teacher reprimanding her students. "When I said I wanted to be kept informed, I meant about each and *every* thing. If I think for one second you're holding out on me, or taking unnecessary risks, I'll pull the plug like that." Destini snapped her fingers. I nodded my understanding.

Good investigators don't like putting all of their cards on the table until they have shored up their hand. Destini knew that. I also knew she would be keeping a close eye on me for a while.

We both leaned back. Destini took her time spreading her cloth napkin over her lap as if she were petting a kitten. "This is what bothers me about bringing you in on any of my cases." Destini stared me square in the eyes. Her statement was peremptory.

"Pardon?"

"You take chances, C. J."

"And you don't."

"At times, it comes with the territory."

"Like going undercover."

"That's rare for homicide detectives and you know it."

"It wouldn't happen at all if you'd say no. It's not like being a homicide detective isn't dangerous enough."

"I don't want to say no. I enjoy going undercover. It breaks the monotony of straight investigative work."

"Did you enjoy being shot at?" It hadn't been the first time Destini had been under fire. My biggest fear was it wouldn't be the last.

"Of course not." Destini's tone suggested I was being ridiculous. "That was over four months ago, and I'm still here. I can't believe you're still harping on that. I would think you'd understand how it is, being a former field operative. Besides, I've been shot at during regular homicide investigations. That doesn't seem to bother you."

I had no rebuttal for her last statement, but I wasn't done. "What I understand, my love, is how dangerous undercover work can be. What I understand is: you could be killed. Which is exactly why I won't—" I stopped myself short of saying it.

"Go on, exactly why you won't what?" We stared defiantly into each other's eyes. Destini leaned forward.

"Let me finish it for you. That's exactly why you won't marry me."

That was it! I thought. That explained why Destini looked so damn good. She was expecting a marriage proposal. What had I done or said to make Destini believe tonight was the night I would pop the question? That was a mystery to which I had no clue.

Our silence spoke volumes. A standoff was brewing. I felt my unreasonable stubbornness kicking in. Destini knew me all too well. She was right on why I was reluctant to marry the woman I loved. I was certain she could see it from the glare in my eyes; the anger on my face. She may have spoken the truth, but I'd be damned if I were going to admit it to her. Our salads arrived. The waiter ended our standoff.

"Let's enjoy our meal," I said, attempting to keep the edge out of my voice. Destini nodded in firm agreement. It took us until the entrée to cool off.

"What about Alice Harriman?" Destini asked. "Think she's involved?"

"Possibly. One thing's for certain. Her grief is real."

"So are most of the killers who do in their spouses."

"Motive."

"You wanted this case raw, remember?"

"I believe it was more like cold."

"Care for a copy of my preliminary report?" Destini asked. She had a wide grin that only vanished when a forkful of Romaine lettuce passed through her lips.

"Not yet. I'm still fishing. I would like to know about the body."

"The medical examiner's findings, you mean?"

"Correct."

"Cause of death was a .22 slug at the base of the skull," Destini said.

"Anything else?" Destini took her time before answering. *Dangling a carrot before me*, I thought.

"The victim had been savagely beaten before his death."

"As if he were being tortured."

"That'd be my guess."

"Possibly for information. They wanted something; something worth a man's life."

I contemplated the varied possibilities surrounding that statement. From my experience, that could be anything from multi-million dollar drug deals to a rock of crack cocaine. I swept my mind clean. It was important that I kept it open to receive only the facts. I gently prodded Destini for more information.

"The house cleaner, Suzanne Kwong, mentioned a diary that Don Harriman kept," I said. "Do you have any such item in your possession?"

"No."

"I may need your help finding it."

"You want me to pay the widow a visit? Ask her about her husband's diary? Because of something you did?" She smiled.

"If you don't mind, I would; but let's just say Alice is not speaking to me at the moment. I want to give her time to cool off. And how'd you know about my standing with the widow?"

"Alice Harriman called me to complain about you. Strange how you have that effect on women."

"What effect?"

"A delightful way of pissing us off." I deflected Destini's comment with a snide grin. "What about the maid?" she asked.

"Suzanne Kwong and Don Harriman were having an affair."

"*Really.*" Destini brightened as if she'd just heard a juicy morsel of office gossip. "That's interesting."

"I'm keeping a lid on it, though."

"Why?"

"I'm confident Suzanne had nothing to do with Harriman's killing."

"Suzanne, huh. Most people call her Suzy."

"She prefers Suzanne."

"She told you that."

"Yep."

"Should I be worried about her stealing you away?" Destini asked with a flirtatious smile. "Or is she only interested in married men?"

"Only if you plan on dumping me for not asking for your hand in marriage tonight, in answer to your first question. If you do dump me, who knows—I might need a shoulder to cry on."

"I thought Renita would be first in line to lend you a shoulder, if needed."

"Whoever's available," I said, continuing to play along.

"I'd pay to see that fight."

"Nobody's fighting over me."

"Not even me." Destini feigned a pout.

"Most especially you; and no, Suzanne isn't only interested in married men."

"There'll come a time when you'll ask for my hand, Cedric Joseph Cavanaugh," Destini said, back to her cool self.

"I have no doubt of that. Will you take my last name when I do?"

"We'll discuss that when the time comes." This time Destini switched topics. "What makes you certain that Suzanne had nothing to do with Don Harriman's disappearance or murder?"

"Their affair was still ongoing. They were never in love with one another. To hear her tell it, it was only a temporary fling. She misses him, but that's it. No jealousy or false expectations."

"You believe her?"

"You interviewed Suzanne. Do you think I should trust her?"

"She was direct and honest as a bullet when I talked to her."

"I would have sought a different metaphor, but that was my impression, as well."

"Sounds like you're off to a good start. I gather Alice Harriman is your prime suspect?"

"For now. I somehow believe she's involved."

"Motive?"

"Nothing concrete."

"What about her husband's affair with Suzanne? That could've triggered what happened?"

"If Alice Harriman knew about the affair. I had the impression she didn't have a clue."

"Why else would a woman kill the man she loves?"

"Good question. Better yet, why the kidnapping; the beating; that whole elaborate mess?"

"Maybe they were supposed to do him at home. Make it look like a robbery."

"Or maybe they were after something Don Harriman wasn't willing to part with."

Destini nodded her agreement. "Where do we go from here?" she said.

"I'll write you a progress report on everything I've learned so far."

"Including the details on your little skirmish?"

Destini put down her fork. She reached over and lightly rubbed my cut knuckle. Her touch was like warm satin. I nodded in answer to her question. Her hand left mine, interlocking with her other fingers beneath her chin. Destini gave me that all-encompassing gaze that only women seem to have mastered. I wondered if there was something in my teeth. Her smile made my stubbornness easier to swallow.

"You're learning," Destini said, resuming her meal. I was confused as to what that meant. Was she referring to her work, her professional expectations, her personal requirements, or something altogether different? I decided to let the matter rest rather than make myself dizzy with the possibilities. My priorities once again shifted. By the end of our date, I was grateful for a goodnight kiss and Destini's thanks for a lovely evening.

CHAPTER FIFTEEN

I hadn't seen much of my partner the day before due to the Harriman case. When I stepped into her office, I found Renita seated behind her desk putting the final touches on our monthly invoices. She asked what was up. I updated her on the Harriman case.

"We're doing the Harriman investigation pro bono?" Renita asked, sealing the last envelope and placing it on a small stack of its cousins, stamped and ready to go.

"Do I have a choice?" I said, half-sitting on her desk.

"It's your call." Renita slipped the stack of envelopes in her backpack, kicked back, and relaxed. "You could turn it down."

"Don't worry, you're still getting paid."

"This I know," Renita said with a smile. Her smile devolved into a grin; a sly, mischievous grin. Something was up.

"What's going on?"

"What makes you think anything's going on?" Her voice was playful. Her eyes alit, Renita put her feet up on her desk.

"Then why are you grinning like the cat that swallowed the canary?"

"How was dinner last night?" The question surprised me.

"Fine," I said, not trying to mask my suspicion.

"Anything special happen?"

"No—and where are you going with this?"

"I'll bet Detective Pendleton looked lovely." Her grin broadened. It was Renita who was behind last night's misunderstanding. In a way, I was relieved. At least I had discovered I wasn't losing my mind when it came to Destini. I tried not to let on I knew what Renita was inferring. It would be better if she told me herself. That way, there would be no misinterpretations.

"Destini always looks lovely to me, Renita."

"How sweet," Renita said, still grinning. Renita put her feet down and leaned forward on the desk. "I'll bet she looked especially lovely last night."

"Yes, she did; and how would you know that?"

"Did you propose?"

"No." After a brief pause, I added: "I forgot the ring." Renita's face went blank.

"*You're kidding*," Renita said, at first uncertain. Gradually, her obnoxious grin returned.

"Obviously, so were you." Her expression turned smug.

"You told Destini I planned to propose to her last night."

"Of course not." Renita feigned seriousness. "I merely implied the possibility that you might ask her to marry you." Her grin once again broadened.

"That wasn't funny, Renita. In fact, it was downright cruel." Renita's attitude changed from amusement to resentment.

"Cruel? What I did was cruel?" Renita stood, her voice building with hostility. "You see how Destini treats me. Always with her smart-ass remarks, bagging on me every chance she gets. It was time for a little payback."

"Destini may treat you a little harsh at times, but she'd never stoop that low. You couldn't simply put salt in her coffee?" I tried to lighten her mood while attempting to placate my irritation at what she'd done.

"Maybe next time," Renita said, with attitude.

"I thought that silly feud between you and Destini was over." Renita looked at me as if I was crazy.

"Whatever gave you that idea?" I couldn't tell Renita about the time I'd eavesdropped on a conversation between her and Destini when Renita agreed to give Destini her respect by backing off. I wondered when that detente dissolved.

"For a while, you two were getting along fine."

"Those days are over. I'm back to trying to get you for myself."

"We've been over this time and time again. That ain't gonna happen," I said with conviction. "And what about Ernest?"

"Say the word and he's history." At seven-three, Ernest Fullman was close to 400 pounds of muscle. Knowing the way Ernest felt about Renita, I could be the one who was history.

"You need to move on."

Renita walked around the desk, positioning herself between my legs. She put her arms around my neck and smiled. In her sweetest voice, Renita said: "You can't blame a woman for trying, sugar."

Our gazes met. What passed between us was electric; the kind of voltage that is generated before a first kiss. I had learned to safeguard myself against allowing situations like that to occur. It wasn't love. It wasn't lust. It was sensuality; the most lethal lure to mature men. I was unprepared for the warm tidal wave of desire that washed over me. I removed Renita's arms from around my neck. With my hands on her waist, I firmly pushed Renita away, giving myself enough room to stand.

"Yes I can, dumpling. We're friends and colleagues. Although I don't know how much longer either relationship is going to last if you keep pulling stunts like that one."

"Friends and lovers; where have I heard that song before?"

"Not in this office."

"You want me to say I'm sorry. Don't you, C. J.?"

"And mean it."

"I apologize."

"Not to me; to Destini."

"Are you crazy? Forget it."

"Let me put it this way," I said with calm precision. "Either you apologize to Destini, or this partnership is dissolved."

The words came out without regret. Renita straightened with her hands on her hips. Her expression was a combination of anger and agony, as if I had told her the worst thing she could imagine times two.

"All right, C. J. I'll do it for you." Her voice was barely a whisper. Renita reached for the phone.

"In person," I said. "Face-to-face."

I thought Renita was going to double over in pain.

"What? When?"

"The sooner, the better."

"Let me get this straight." Her cocky attitude returned for a moment. "You want me to go to the police station and apologize to Destini?"

"Yes. Maybe then you'll understand how humiliated Destini felt."

"I said I was sorry." Renita's voice was as close to a plea as she was capable.

"Do it, Renita. I'm not playing."

"I don't know if I can." Renita looked on the verge of passing out. It didn't matter. She had crossed the line. Nobody treated Destini that way; not even one of my dearest and trusted friends.

"If you don't do it, start packing."

I escaped to my office, busying myself with paperwork. A few minutes later, I saw Renita make her way out the front door as if she were part of a funeral procession. I watched Renita leave, feeling no sympathy toward her. Had I been that forceful sooner, maybe things wouldn't have gone that far. Perhaps it was time to reassess the dynamics of our partnership.

CHAPTER SIXTEEN

Derek Knopp was dead. According to his doctor, serious complications had developed due to the severity of his burns. Bacterial pneumonia set in, to make a long explanation short. There was nothing the doctor could do. Derek Knopp drowned from a sudden heavy buildup of fluid in his lungs.

I telephoned Renita from my car phone to tell her about Knopp. The Fire Marshall had called. He informed Renita he had emailed me a copy of the report on the Knopp fire. If I had any questions, I could give him a call. I headed back to the office to have a look at the report.

Renita was gone when I returned to the office. She had taken a late lunch with Ernest, according to her text message. I disregarded the additional comment for me not to be jealous and her closing of "XOXOXO, Renita." Obviously, our little chat on professional boundaries had proven useless. Things were back to normal for us.

According to the Incident/Offense Report Case Number 19-2017, collected samples from the house fire had been sent to the state crime lab. The lab determined a petroleum distillate (gasoline) was used as a catalyst in the Knopp fire. Preliminary analysis on the basement samples suggested it had been burned prior to the fire that destroyed the house. They were still conducting tests on those samples. There was no speculation on Derek Knopp. It was not their job to investigate or make determinations. The Fire Marshall did unofficially state some of his opinions in his email.

The Fire Marshall suspected Mr. Knopp was a bit too generous with the accelerant. It probably caused the house to go up a lot faster than Knopp expected. The Fire Marshall wouldn't have been surprised if Derek Knopp hadn't accidentally gotten some of the gasoline on himself. A quick call to Knopp's doctor confirmed the Fire Marshall's last suspicion.

I put in an email request to Carl Wheaton at Lunsford Insurance for Don and Alice Harriman's personal and business insurance files. Then I wrote the progress report on the Harriman case that I had promised Destini and emailed it to her at the precinct.

Mapping out the Harriman case gave me an opportunity to summarize where I stood.

What I had so far was a man who was, in actuality, Don Harriman; but who had introduced himself to me as Barrette Wells. That same man had an affair with his house cleaner, Suzanne Kwong. Don Harriman was also a business partner with his wife, Alice Harriman, for less than three years in the most lucrative real estate firm in the Pacific Northwest. Don Harriman had kept a personal diary that had yet to turn up. Harriman had been kidnapped, beaten, and then murdered over something he either possessed or knew or both. And finally, Don Harriman had, for some unknown reason, sent me a text message that, for the time being, meant nothing.

I plugged the synopsis into the computer SUMMARY file folder I kept under HARRIMAN. No sooner had I finished than Renita returned from lunch. After Renita fed me the details of her wonderful lunch and I calmed her down from her flirting, we updated one another on our business day. Our final discussion centered on how we would proceed on the Harriman case.

CHAPTER SEVENTEEN

One area I had overlooked were the people who were on the scene right after Suzanne's cry for help, the neighbors—they had been there—particularly the two who went inside the Harriman home to investigate. Perhaps they could shed some light on the events surrounding Don Harriman's abduction.

I began with the neighbor that lived on the west side of Alice Harriman. Janice Bigelow was in her early thirties, about five seven, and even in a jogging suit and running shoes, Ms. Bigelow appeared as though she had stepped out of the pages of a department store catalog. Her skin was freckled brown and radiant, giving one the impression she was either tanning or that her tan was fading. Ms. Bigelow had wavy brunette hair, high cheekbones, and expressive dark brown eyes.

I introduced myself and briefly explained why I was there. To my surprise, my presence was met with enthusiasm rather than steely circumspection, as I had expected. Janice Bigelow invited me in for a cup of tea.

The colors, patterns, and decor of her house all stated that a woman lived there. Feminine touches were everywhere. 'Dainty' would describe much of it, if that word weren't out of vogue. New Age music played throughout the house, creating a serene environment. She returned with two cups of chamomile tea sweetened with a teaspoon of natural clover honey. Ms. Bigelow made herself comfortable next to me on her country-style sofa after making certain I was attended to. The tea was delicious.

"Ms. Bigelow—"

"Call me Jan. Everyone else does."

We'll see how long that lasts, I thought. Like Suzanne, Jan appeared to be more of a Janice to me. In my opinion, calling her Jan did not demean her womanhood. Jan continued before I could begin my questioning.

"Can you believe what happened to Don? Being kidnapped and murdered in his own home—*and poor Alice*. I don't know how she stays in that house after what's happened. I would have moved out by now. I would think that would be easy for Alice to arrange, being in real estate."

The timbre of her voice was soft and unassuming; almost hypnotic. You had the firm impression it was that way because Jan wanted it that way, not because she was shy or lacked self-confidence. However, I wasn't interested in Jan's conjectures on the lives of Don and Alice Harriman. I politely nodded and moved the inquiry along.

"Where were you when Don Harriman was kidnapped?" I asked.

"Right here, working. I work out of my home. I'm part owner of Nature's Castle. Most of our orders come via the internet. I process the orders here. Once the client's payment has cleared, I send the information on to our warehouse and they ship the products, quick and simple. Have you heard of us?"

"You deal in vitamins, minerals, oils, teas—goods of that sort." I took a sip of tea, followed immediately by another.

"Those and a whole lot more. The difference with us is that all of our products are 100 percent natural like our name, Nature's Castle. Let me get you one of our catalogs." Before I could dissuade Jan, she darted out of sight, returning moments later with a fistful of magazine-size catalogs. In an unfair exchange, I gave Jan one of my business cards.

"Here you go." She thrust the catalogs at me with both hands. For the first time, I noticed her fingers—long and slender, like her body, and well kept. Jan appeared to have never known manual labor; not that I had expected her to. She also lacked the arrogance of the silver spoon crowd. That placed her in the middle-class echelon; a position in society from which access to white collar, blue collar and blue blood communities are available. Jan returned to her spot on the sofa.

"Share the others with your friends," she said. "I guarantee you'll find something in there you can use."

I thanked her, placing the catalogs beside my tea on the walnut coffee table. "You were home at the time of the kidnapping?"

"As near as I can figure. When we—"

"We?" I asked.

"Myself and Lock."

"Lock?" Even though I knew two people had entered the Harriman residence on the day of the kidnapping, I always found it best to allow witnesses the freedom to divulge as much information as possible. It gave me an opportunity to compare notes with what I knew and what I learned.

"John Ullock," Jan said. "Everyone calls him Lock. He lives on the other side of Alice." I made a mental note of his name. "When we went inside, we didn't see anything."

"What happened before that?"

"Before what?"

"What happened to bring you outside of your home?"

"Oh! I heard someone screaming for help."

"You immediately rushed outside?"

"Yes."

"The person you're referring to is the house cleaner?"

"Yes. I don't know her name."

I saw no reason to tell her Suzanne Kwong's name. Jan continued.

"Lock was with her by the time I got there."

"Then what happened?"

"We were able to get from the house cleaner what had her so upset. Two men with guns were going to kill Don."

"The two of you went inside to check it out."

"Yes."

"What did you find?"

"Nothing; nothing at all. Everything looked normal to us."

"Weren't you frightened?"

"Frightened of what?"

"Entering a possibly dangerous situation. I mean, that took some guts. I would've been concerned even if I had a weapon. But you and Lock walked right in without giving it a second thought." Jan sipped her tea, not in the least affected by my assertion.

"I suppose," she said. "I really didn't give it much thought at the time. I mean, that poor girl was scared. What else could we do?"

"You could've waited for the police like the rest of your neighbors."

Jan paused for a thoughtful moment, taking a sip of her tea. I did the same. "It must have been that adrenaline rush," Jan said.

"Adrenaline rush?" I was uncertain what Jan was getting at.

"Like the one I get when I skydive or when I'm dirt biking. You don't think. You react. Do you know what I mean?" Her smile was sly, as if she were sharing a dirty little secret. I was surprised to hear that Jan skydived or

79

dirt biked. Jan struck me as a hiker or camper; a getting in touch with nature type of person or a Greenpeace member; not a thrill seeker.

"Yes, I do." I did know what Jan meant; but not from recreational hobbies. My adrenaline rushes came from being placed in dangerous situations not often of my own choosing.

"I have to confess that I didn't believe the house cleaner at first," Jan said. "As I said: when we went in, we found no—how would you put it— evidence?"

I nodded.

"We found no evidence anything had happened." Once again, I moved the inquiry along.

"Do you remember anything different or strange when you were inside the Harriman house?" I said.

Slowly shaking her head, Jan thought for a moment. "Nothing comes to mind. Sorry. But I couldn't be certain. I've only been in Alice's house a few times."

"How long have you known the Harrimans?" I said, finishing off my tea.

"Ever since I moved in. That's been about a year and a half."

"Have you noticed anything odd or unusual that went on over there?"

"No," Jan said with a smirk. "To be honest, they were pretty quiet; kept to themselves. Most people do in this neighborhood. You know your neighbors' faces and names and pick up on a little gossip here and there, but it typically doesn't go any further than that. People are too busy, I suppose."

I nodded in agreement.

I had a second and third cup of tea while Jan told me her life story, including why and how she and a college girlfriend started Nature's Castle. Intriguing as it was, it didn't bring me any closer to Don Harriman's killers. It wasn't a total loss in that regard. I did leave with some complimentary Nature's Castle teas and an 8-ounce jar of their all-natural clover honey.

CHAPTER EIGHTEEN

"Who is it?" A gruff, husky voice said through the hardwood door. I identified myself. "What do you want?" came the response.

"I was wondering if I could ask you a few questions about what happened to Don Harriman," I said in my most non-threatening voice. The door cracked open. A pasty, pudgy face with a 2-inch reddish scar on his left cheek and drowsy dark blue eyes stared out at me.

"John Ullock?" I asked.

"You got any ID?" I showed him my photo PI license. He opened the door, turned, and walked away. "Close the door behind you," he said, not looking back.

About in his early thirties, five eight and 220 pounds was the potbellied man I followed into the living room. His dark blond hair was tied back into a thin ponytail, adversely emphasizing his drastically receding hairline. He wore square-toed leather boots, a bolo tie, a western-styled shirt, and dark blue jeans that looked to be a size too small. His handcrafted silver belt buckle strained to be seen from beneath his belly. On his chubby right pinky, forefinger, and ring fingers he wore large gold, opal, and platinum rings. On his chubby left forefinger and ring fingers he wore large ruby and turquoise rings. A large diamond earring erupted from a thick right earlobe.

The place could have used Sparkling Palace Maid Service as well as an interior decorator. It smelled of cigar smoke, sweat, fried foods, and decaying garbage. To call it a pigsty would have been an insult to pigs. All of the furnishings looked as though they had been purchased on the last day of a garage sale, and without any sense of coordination. The man signaled for me to sit on his olive green corduroy couch. I brushed away what looked to be potato chip droppings and did so. He sat in his brown leather recliner, popped up the footrest, and made himself comfortable. The TV was on. Jerry Springer. He muted the sound, reached over to the TV tray to his right, and grabbed a perspiring can of Miller Lite. At his other elbow was a matching TV tray. On that TV tray, a smoldering green leafed cigar, as fat as one of his fingers, lay in the round notch of a gaudy glass ashtray littered with cigar butts. He flicked the ashes off his cigar into the ashtray, took a long drag, and asked how he could help me.

"Are you John Ullock?"

"That's me." He sounded as though he were amused by my question.

"Mr. Ullock—"

"What's this 'Mr. Ullock' shit?" he interrupted. "Call me Lock." He smiled, displaying his tobacco-and-coffee stained teeth. His statement lacked sincerity, sounding rehearsed.

"How long have you known the Harrimans, Lock?"

Lock looked toward the ceiling for a moment, then back at me. "Since I moved in."

"Do you get along with them as neighbors?"

"*Hell yeah.* Goddamn shame what happened. Goes to show you anything's possible at any time in this crazy world we live in." Lock squirmed in his seat, appearing to be feeling for the sweet spot in his recliner. He settled in once he found it.

"What kind of neighbors were the Harrimans?"

"Quiet, private; no trouble to me. What's your stake in this?"

"I've been asked to help out the police on this particular investigation."

"I didn't know the cops needed help doing their job."

"Normally they don't; but occasionally they ask for outside consultants to step in."

"You must be damn good."

"I'm not bad."

"How much do you charge?"

"It depends on the case. If you don't mind, could you answer my question?"

"Which question's that?"

"What kind of neighbors were the Harrimans?"

"We hardly said more than the usual pleasantries to each other. You know: good morning, how are you, nice day, crappy day, shit like that. Although I have to admit that Alice is a hot tamale. Think I've got a chance now that she's a widow?" Lock winked at me.

Maybe in hell, I thought. "I have no idea," I said, keeping the amusement I felt from his last statement out of my voice.

Lock took a healthy swallow of beer followed by a long drag of his cigar. An enormous cloud of blue smoke billowed toward the ceiling when he exhaled, not making much of a difference to the already stale hazy air.

"Can you tell me in your own words what happened on the day Don Harriman was kidnapped?" I said.

"Who else's words would I use?" Lock chuckled.

"Right," I said, forcing a smile.

"I'm working when I hear someone screaming their head off," Lock said. "I run outside to see what the hell's going on. Get out there, and this little Asian chick in a maid's uniform is screaming her lungs out."

I couldn't imagine John Ullock running anywhere for any reason. "The Asian chick you're referring to was the house cleaner?"

"Didn't I just say she was wearing a maid's uniform?"

"Right, go on."

"I get out there and she's all hysterical. Babbling on about some men and Don—I didn't know what the hell she was talking about. Jan calmed her down enough for us to figure out what she was saying."

"Jan," I said, once again applying my unwritten rule of an eyewitness account juxtaposed against previously ascertained information.

"Jan Bigelow. She lives on the other side of Alice. Now, there's another hot tamale I'd like to give a ride on the big salami, if you know what I mean?" Lock grinned salaciously, sipped his beer, and puffed on his cigar. The cigar was four-fifths done. He ground it out and lit another. I ignored his last statement and urged Lock to continue with his account.

"Yeah," Lock said. "While this chick is going on about someone going to kill Don, I told one of the neighbors to call the cops."

Katherine Hall was the neighbor who had made the call to the police. She died just a few days after the incident. The ME confirmed the doctor's report that her death was due to sudden cardiac arrest. No foul play was detected. I did a background check on the woman most people called Katie, as standard procedure. Aside from a couple of college student arrests for participating in unauthorized campus protests and a few parking and speeding tickets, her record was clean. Katie was a retired college physics professor who was active in volunteer and charity work. A widower, she left behind three children and two grandkids. She was only sixty-five years old.

"…Then Jan and I go in to see what's going on."

"Inside the Harriman house," I said.

"That's what we're talking about, ain't it?" Lock sounded annoyed, then looked embarrassed—I assumed because he probably prided himself on maintaining control. He righted himself and finished his story.

"That was brave of you, Lock." I attempted to sound sincere. It apparently worked. Lock poked out his flabby chest and straightened a little in his chair.

"How so?" he said.

"Going into an unknown situation against armed men."

Lock took a drag of his cigar. "You gotta do what you gotta do. Besides, I had my Peacemaker with me to help even the score."

"You own a Colt Single Action Army revolver?"

"*No.* It's a Remington .45 automatic. You wanna see it?"

"I'm good, thanks. The place was deserted when you went in?"

"Like a whorehouse on Sunday morning." Lock chuckled at his own joke.

"Any sign of a struggle? Did anything look out of place?"

"No men, no Don, no struggle, no nothing."

"You sound disappointed."

"It's been a long time since I've been in a good fight. I was ready."

I was curious if Lock had ever been involved in a gunfight. My instincts told me he hadn't. Most people who had weren't itching for another.

"Somehow those men must have gotten away," I said. I was hoping Lock might be able to lend some insight on how that could have happened.

"If they were ever there."

"What are you trying to say?"

"I'm saying that sweet little Asian chick might've been in on the whole deal."

This guy was really annoying, but I had to play along. "Do you have any evidence to support your theory?"

"Look at the facts."

"That's what I'm here for: the facts."

"Well, here they are," Lock said, as though about to spell things out so even a dimwit like me could understand. "Don disappears, right. Kidnapped by two dudes who nobody but little Miss Cutie saw. Next thing you know, Don shows up dead. You do the math."

"And her motive is?"

"The great motivator: money, of course."

"There was no ransom request. No money was paid."

"The whole thing backfired and they had to whack the poor bastard. It happens. If I were you, I'd be setting my sights on that hot little Asian maid. She knows the score, believe me."

A slob, an idiot, and a chauvinist, I thought. No wonder the Harrimans kept their distance from this man.

Lock took a couple of drags from his cigar and a deep swallow of beer. "Anyway, that's my objective opinion. Take it for it's worth."

You need to look up the word 'objective', I thought. Once again, I moved the inquiry along. "You work at home?"

"Mostly. I'm a pharmaceutical supplier—hospitals, drug store chains, supermarket chains—the works. The Big Lock does 'em all. I've got a client list as long as your arm. They call, text, or email their orders. I pass the orders along to a reputable distributor. Follow up to make certain everything went okay on the client's end. And that's that. Occasionally I have to make a site visit. But for the most part, my ass is planted in that office."

Lock pointed with his cigar hand toward the one room I could see that looked as though it had been recently cleaned. "God bless the Internet." Lock raised his beer in a toast before taking a swallow.

"Want a beer?" Lock said, with a flash of manners.

"No thanks. Who do you work for, Lock?"

"I'm an independent contractor. What that means is I work for myself. The client informs me of their needs. I find them the best deals and place their orders."

"Sounds challenging."

"Sometimes yes, sometimes no. When you have as many connections as I do, it makes things a whole lot easier." Lock took a couple of long drags, flicked off the ashes in the ashtray, and then took another drag.

John Ullock almost never took his eyes off me from the moment I sat down. He was studying me. I presumed it was his habit. Having a salesman's mentality, he was probably accustomed to sizing up people in a hurry. I wondered how he read me at that moment (not that I cared about his personal assessment). But it was always good to know your opponent's tactics in such matters. It helped control your investigation by expediting your victories over them. And, for the time being, I did regard John Ullock as an opponent.

Lock was about to expound on his theory of Ms. Kwong's guilt when I cut him short. I told him I had pressing business I needed to attend to. Lock seemed disappointed, but understood.

I handed Lock one of my business cards and gave him my standard investigator statement that if he remembered anything else, he should give me a call. We shook hands in parting. His hand was clammy. Was that normal, or was Lock nervous? Only time would tell. I thought about dropping Mavis Gutterson a line on behalf of The Big Lock—prick Mavis with the idea of giving Lock a free 30-day trial service. That might reel in a new client for Mavis and make up for my deceiving her. Not to mention getting John Ullock a new lease on cleanliness.

I spent the rest of the day canvassing Crystal Gardens. No one saw anything, heard anything, or knew anything prior to Suzanne's outburst. Everything after that was third-or fourth-hand speculation.

One new fact did surface, which was unwittingly collaborated by everyone I interviewed after John Ullock: he did not tell anyone to call the police. Katherine Hall volunteered to do that on her own. Lock could have been mistaken about making the demand. Intense moments can affect our memories in a way that distorts accurate recollection. Add Lock's ego to that and it could have been a subconscious addition to bolster his rep. My instincts told me that wasn't the case.

I noticed that something was missing, on my way to my car. There were no signs of anyone staking out Alice Harriman's house. Maybe it was because Alice Harriman wasn't home. Maybe it was because of what went down between me, Al, and Tadpole. Or maybe it was because Al was lying about why he and Tadpole were there in the first place.

CHAPTER NINETEEN

Don Harriman didn't have a life insurance policy with Lunsford Insurance, according to the email response from Carl Wheaton—not even through his company, Blue Sun. Don Harriman didn't have a life insurance policy with any insurance company as far as Carl Wheaton knew. He did have health insurance coverage through Blue Sun. Even that was part of an umbrella HMO. While his lack of life insurance raised suspicions, Carl would not release the private insurance documents of Don or Alice Harriman.

I gave Carl a call. Try as I might, Carl wouldn't budge on that issue. Carl Wheaton was by the book, if nothing else. The Harrimans were not under investigation by Lunsford Insurance; therefore, their files were inaccessible to The Cavanaugh Investigation Agency. There was a catch. The Knopp fire was a Blue Sun property. Carl bit on that morsel of justification. Carl emailed us what he deemed appropriate. That was going out on a limb for Carl.

Renita and I poured over the data, searching for anything that might prove suspicious or enlightening. The information Carl sent us consisted of full names, birthdays, social security numbers, places of birth, home and business addresses, home and business telephone numbers, etcetera, etcetera. Basic information you could find on any American citizen in a few hours. That meant Renita and I would have to utilize other resources to uncover detailed background intelligence on the Harrimans.

The rain had returned, ending a consecutive string of sunny spring days. It was perfect timing for the grunt work we needed to do. Renita and I split up the files. Renita took Alice Harriman, leaving me with the corpse.

CHAPTER TWENTY

Guile is part and parcel to an investigator no matter what anyone says. It's your trump card. Whether it is referred to as misdirection, deception, deceit, double-dealing, treachery, cheating, or cunning, it all flows back to the same ocean. Results are what you're after. Sometimes a little guile can go a long way toward that goal.

The information Carl Wheaton had emailed us provided enough leads for in-depth inquirers. Renita and I spent most of that day, and all of the next, on the telephone.

It doesn't take much to gain a person's confidence over the telephone. Using a form of deception known in the intelligence community as Social Engineering, Renita and I were able to gather background information on the Harrimans.

Donald Farrell Harriman was born in Baltimore, Maryland; the only child of Bernice Harriman, a single mother who bounced around during his formative years. The Harrimans eventually settled in Lincoln, Nebraska where Don graduated high school, an average student, well liked and trouble-free. After graduation, Don enlisted in the Army. Following a less than remarkable career in the Armed Forces, Don attended the University of Cincinnati, where he earned a degree in International Finance. From there, Don went to work for a bank, then a finance company, then a traditional brokerage; finally settling in with Trumbull, a national real estate firm.

A heavy smoker, Bernice Harriman died after an extended bout with inoperable lung cancer. Don took a leave of absence from Trumbull to grieve the loss of his only known relative. Don extended that leave to earn a degree in Real Estate Law. Harriman returned to Trumbull after acquiring his second degree. Trumbull offered Don a vice-president position with their Seattle office. Harriman accepted the position and, as Alice Harriman had said, Seattle was where he met his wife.

Don joined Blue Sun Real Estate as the executive Vice President of Finance. Alice and Don were married shortly thereafter; a marriage going on two-and-a-half years. Don became the other half of Blue Sun Real Estate and Blue Sun Construction Services. That was where his life came to a screeching halt.

The murder victim was ambitious, conscientious, dependable, and fair, by all accounts. What was missing from his biography was data surrounding his personal life. Who were his friends, ex-girlfriends, colleagues? What memberships did he have? To what associations and fraternity did he belong? What were his hobbies, quirks, habits? No one seemed to know. Everyone I spoke with said Don kept to himself, vehemently guarded his privacy, and had no hobbies or eccentricities they could recall. That left a gaping hole in the picture. Our social, more than our professional, connections inform people about who we are. Don Harriman's personal life was a closed book; one that I needed to pry open and read.

"Alicia Michelle Baker was born in Seattle to Perry and Marsha," Renita reported. "Third child of two brothers and three sisters. Alice—as everyone called Alicia—was reared in Bellingham, Washington. A straight A student, valedictorian and high school track star, Alice was both popular and respected by peers and faculty alike. Those qualities carried over to Washington State University, where she turned down an academic scholarship for an athletic one. That turned out to be a big mistake. Alice faired far better in the classroom than she did on the track.

"Graduating with high honors and a business degree, Alice Baker went on to manage a Nike sporting goods store. After working a year, Alice attended the University of Washington to earn a Master's Degree in Business. From there, Alice accepted a managerial position with a major bank for six months, quitting to take on the Northwest Zone Director's position with a fast-charging real estate firm.

"Having earned a stellar reputation for being intelligent, aggressive, focused, and visionary, Alice moved quickly through the ranks and was awarded the presidency of the Seattle office in just three years. Shortly thereafter, Alice decided to branch out on her own. Alicia Michelle Baker opened Blue Sun Real Estate. Within six years, Blue Sun became the largest Real Estate firm in the entire Pacific Northwest.

"Unlike her husband, Alice Baker had a long, impressive list of affiliations. She was a licensed broker in all of the northwestern states. Her professional memberships, associations, accreditations and certifications were with reputable and noted national, local, and regional financial and real estate organizations. Either through Blue Sun or personally, Alice supported charities such as The Hutchinson Cancer Research Center, the Children's Miracle Network, Junior Achievement, Big Brothers, Big Sisters, and National Multiple Sclerosis. Alice volunteered for charity work whenever possible, and sponsored her own breast cancer race for The Cure in Bellingham, Washington.

"On a personal note, Alice Baker never joined a sorority. Her romantic count was two high school boyfriends, three college boyfriends, and two boyfriends, before she met Don. Her closest friendships were with a couple of girls who attended high school with Alice. The girls no longer lived in the Pacific Northwest. It had been years since they had heard from Alice. One thing both remembered about Alice was a little detail when it came to boys. They described her as being reserved at times—almost bashful—around bright, good-looking boys. Alice was prone to fall in love rather easily with them.

"Like that was news," Renita interjected. "A lot of women have a weakness for that sort of man."

I ignored my partner's little sidebar and motioned for her to move along with her report.

"Since high school, Alice had no close friends. She enjoyed jogging, Judo, tennis, working out, white water rafting, camping, hiking, computer games and bicycling. She wasn't much for small talk, had a weakness for German chocolate cake, and had a scathing temper if you pressed the wrong button.

"According to a former college roommate, during her junior year at WASSAU, Alice was busted, along with two other students, for possession and use of marijuana by campus security. WASSAU campus security had no record of such a bust. Her ex-roommate explained that because Alice was on the track team and it was her first offense, she was released with a verbal warning. When asked about the other two students, her ex-roommate didn't know who they were, and Alice never told her. According to her ex-roommate, Alice didn't drink alcohol nor care for narcotics. But Alice did enjoy an occasional joint, and continued to light up even after the bust." (An engaging tidbit Renita and I were certain Alice Harriman would like to have buried.)

"Are you thinking what I'm thinking?" I asked Renita when she was done.

"You think Don Harriman hustled Alice Baker?"

"Could be. Harriman did use an alias when we met. We need more on Harriman's personal history. Get an idea if Harriman was a womanizer or a con artist."

"He certainly was an adulterer, if that's any help." I agreed.

"Order high school and college yearbooks on Don Harriman."

"Will do. What about Alice Harriman?"

"No need, her past is wide open. What we need on Alice is more of the present."

"Anything else?"

Renita and I had come away with far more questions than answers. The grunt work had only begun.

"Infiltration or reconnaissance?" I asked.

Renita thought for a moment. "I don't know. They're both challenging."

I took a quarter out of my pocket and flipped it high in the air. "Call it," I said before it landed in my right palm.

"Heads."

I slapped the quarter down on the desk. When I lifted my hand, it was tails.

"I'll take infiltration," I said.

Renita asked to see the quarter. Once satisfied there wasn't anything funny about the coin, Renita said: "Suits me. I'll get on reconnaissance first thing tomorrow."

"Start with Blue Sun's major competitors. See if there are any serious rifts between them and the Harrimans."

"What, exactly, are we looking for?"

"Let's just say a loophole to hang a murderer."

"If nothing turns up?"

"Then trickle down; go to work on the smaller fish: associates, partners—"

"The gardener, the plumber, the butcher, the baker, the candlestick maker." We both laughed about Renita's last three mentions.

"Leave them to me," I said. "I'll handle anyone who's been within their circle of late. You stay on the perimeter."

"So if I would've chosen reconnaissance, you would have tried to talk me out of it."

"Bingo."

"Are you worried about me, C. J.?" Renita's bedroom voice had found its way into our professional dialogue.

"You can't be too careful when killers are involved," I said, maintaining a business tone.

Renita leaned forward, licked her lips, sensually smiled, and then said, "How about you and I have dinner at my place tonight? You can protect me from those big, bad killers."

"And who will protect me from you?"

"Sugar, there's nothing I'd do to you that a man would need protection from."

I snapped my fingers. Renita was startled.

"Dinner," I said. "That reminds me." I picked up the telephone and called Destini. It was her turn to make dinner. While Destini convinced me she was too busy to make dinner, Renita became annoyed and left in a huff. Destini and I agreed to dine at my place.

Adultery was the only visible motive we had for Don Harriman's murder, despite all we'd learned. Even that was a flimsy consideration, given that Alice Harriman didn't appear to know anything about her husband's affair with Suzanne Kwong. If Alice Harriman had discovered his infidelity, she didn't strike me as the type of woman who would hire someone to kill her husband. I believed Alice would have shot Don on the spot, from what little I'd seen of her temper. If Alice Harriman wasn't behind Don Harriman's death, then who was?

CHAPTER TWENTY-ONE

I had decided to refocus the Harriman investigation on the two kidnappers. There wasn't much to go on: white males, one blue-eyed, the other brown-eyed; both wearing blue jeans, denim jackets, turtlenecks, ski masks, work gloves and tan leather work boots. The boots and gloves suggested they were laborers; maybe even construction workers. My gut told me they worked for Blue Sun Construction Services. I needed a list of BSCS employees to narrow my search. There were two legal ways I could obtain that list. One was to go through Alice Harriman.

Destini reneged on speaking to Alice Harriman. She said it was my case until she said otherwise, and it was up to me to smooth out bumps of my own creation. I'm sure that was her way of paying me back for not having proposed. I thanked her for nothing.

When I walked into the executive suite of Blue Sun Enterprises, Alice Harriman was standing at the front desk, talking to a woman of average height, in her early forties, with dark, shiny hair and clear blue eyes, wearing a sleeveless black wool dress and a tasteful string of pearls. Her name was Charlotte Dolman, according to the nameplate. I soon learned she was Alice Harriman's Personal Assistant.

Alice Harriman was a different woman from the one I'd originally met. A teal, double-breasted business suit, a crisp white cotton shirt, and black open-toed pumps had replaced the thick cotton bathrobe and fuzzy house slippers. Her color had returned, giving her a rosy complexion. Her eyes, once red and puffy, were a brisk, clear brown. Her tousled brunette hair had been styled into a glossy layered shoulder cut that framed her oval face. Modest touches of makeup highlighted without becoming overbearing. Her rounded chin jutted slightly forward. A pinched, upturned nose moved away from her thin lips.

Alice Harriman stood erect, with a confident visage. She was a striking woman blessed with brains and power: a fusion that some men found alluring, others intoxicating, and other men feared. I was obviously a member of the second group. Destini was proof of that.

"What do you want, Cavanaugh?" Alice Harriman said. Her voice was sharp; the tone commanding.

"Once again, I want to offer my condolences for the loss of your husband. And I was wondering if I might have a word with you in private?"

"I'm busy," Alice snapped as if that should end the matter. For someone trying to help, I certainly was receiving the cold shoulder a lot.

"I can do this without you, Mrs. Harriman," I calmly said. "One way or another, I'm going to accomplish my objective. Your choice is whether you're interested in being a part of it or not."

Alice Harriman glared at me. I wasn't certain whether it was due to the implication she didn't want to aid in finding her husband's killer, or my impertinence. I wasn't bluffing, in either case. I stared back at her. Her PA looked as though she would like nothing better than to escape. Alice's expression went from scorn to anger.

"Step into my office," the widow Harriman snapped, leading the way. Over her shoulder, she said: "No interruptions, Charlotte." Charlotte Dolman looked away from me when I walked by her, as if embarrassed about something. I followed her boss back to her office.

Alice Harriman's office could comfortably house a family of four. It was bright and spacious, with modern furnishings and all the amenities. Alice closed the door behind us, stepped confidently around her large marble desk, and, in what appeared to be a rehearsed manner, graciously gestured for me to sit across from her in a comfortable black leather chair before seating herself.

Alice looked very cozy in the seat of power. She was tough; no doubt about that. You had to be to thrive in the real estate game. Alice enjoyed her position; enjoyed having power. Then, don't we all?

"My attorney says I don't have to talk to you."

"I never said you did, Mrs. Harriman." I found it interesting she had spoken to her attorney regarding me, at all. It made me wonder what the specifics of the conversation had entailed.

"I'm taking back my maiden name of Baker. And you can call me Ms."

There was a disquieting pause. I let it drift with the current.

"What do you want, Cavanaugh?"

"Information on your BSCS employees."

"What sort of information?"

"I need the names of every white male BSCS employee with blue and brown eyes."

"You're kidding?" Alice said with a girlish smile; one that belied her corporate heart.

"I'm afraid not."

"And why do you need such a list?"

"That's the only description of the kidnapers I have to go on."

"What makes you think these men work for me?"

"A hunch."

"A hunch?" Alice leaned back in her high-backed white leather chair. The smile had vanished, but the amusement lingered in her eyes. She pressed one of the buttons on her speakerphone. The voice of her PA responded.

"Get me a list of all current white male BSCS employees with blue and brown eyes," Alice said.

"Excuse me?" the PA said. Alice repeated her request.

"Right away." The PA hung up.

Alice shut off the speakerphone by pressing the same button. "This may take a few minutes."

"I'll wait."

"You actually believe my husband's killer could be one of my employees?" Her interest appeared genuine. The amusement faded from her eyes.

"It's worth investigating." After a beat, I asked: "Did your husband have a personal assistant?"

"He did."

"I would like to talk to that person."

Alice Baker pressed the same button on her speakerphone as before and ordered her PA to add Joseph Field's home and office number to my list of requests. There was another pause while Alice seemed to mull over the possibility of her husband's murderer working for her. I decided to make the most of our time together.

"What made a born and bred Washingtonian settle in Oregon?" I nonchalantly asked.

"You've been researching me. You're not the police. What gives you the right to pry into my background?" Alice's voice had an irritated tone, but her face held a curious expression. I accepted her expression more than her tone as an ephemeral shift in her attitude toward me. Was her fluctuating interest brought about by my long shot request? The possibility I might actually catch her husband's killer? Or was it something else? I was still trying to determine when Alice Baker was lying. Nothing had broken free. She was still very much a mystery.

"I wouldn't be doing my job if I didn't," I said in response to her question.

"What, exactly, is your job in this matter, Cavanaugh? You were a little ambiguous the last time we spoke." The irritation was gone from her voice. Curiosity had taken center stage.

"Finding your husband's killer. I thought I made that clear."

"I'm all for that. I'm still perplexed why the police would need the assistance of a detective to help apprehend my husband's murderer."

"I volunteered my services. They were accepted." *True enough*, I thought. Filling Alice in on the details wasn't necessary.

"You're actually getting a better deal, Ms. Baker," I continued. "All homicide detectives have more than one case on their docket. Your husband's murder is receiving both police and individual attention."

"I'm flattered," Alice said, not masking her cynicism.

Alice Baker wasn't buying it; at least, not everything. Winning her trust wasn't going to happen. Perhaps it was due to a lingering bad first impression. On the other hand, maybe it was simply the usual disdain private investigators are often met with for meddling in affairs where people felt they didn't belong. Whatever the verdict, Ms. Baker wasn't having any part of yours truly.

"Am I a suspect?" The question was dryly stated. A cunning steeliness had emerged; the cool, calculating mind of a Chairperson of the Board. There was no emotion to be read from her eyes or her face. Alice had switched to business mode.

"I wouldn't call you a suspect, Ms. Baker," I said. "My job is to look at all the possibilities."

"What would you call me?"

"Part of the process of elimination."

"To answer your question," Alice said, "I moved to Oregon to further solidify our market here and to oversee some new construction projects. I have residences and offices in a number of Pacific Northwest locations. It just so happens the Portland area needs my attention most, at present. But I bet you already knew that."

I did. The telephone chirped. Alice Harriman pressed a button and spoke: "Yes."

"The list you requested is ready, Ms. Baker," Charlotte Dolman said.

"Thank you. Mr. Cavanaugh will pick it up on his way out."

I stood to leave. I had felt compassion for Alice Harriman. Alice Baker was a different story. Whatever sense of loss Alice Harriman had for her husband, I believed Alice Baker was over. For Alice Baker, it was back to business as usual.

Halfway to the door, I turned to ask, "Did you know your husband kept a diary?" Shock flickered across her face. I would have missed it if I hadn't been poised for a reaction. Her eyes narrowed slightly along with the tightening of her jaws.

"Yes, I knew Don kept a diary. Who told you?" Her voice didn't change. Alice maintained a flat business tone. I ignored her question. As much as possible, I wanted to shield Suzanne Kwong. My concern was that Alice Baker would deduce my source for herself.

"You'd be surprised what I know, Ms. Baker."

"Not anymore, Cavanaugh. Not anymore."

"May I see the diary?"

Her jaws relaxed. "I don't know where it is."

"It's not in his desk in the study?"

Her eyes narrowed a bit more. "It could be. I'll take a look when I get home."

I believed Ms. Baker didn't have the diary. I also believed she didn't know where it was. Just as I suspected that diary contained a lot of answers to the reason for Don Harriman's kidnapping and execution.

"Will you give me a call if you find it?" I asked.

"Certainly—likewise, I would expect."

I nodded. Neither of us believed the other. I picked up the list from the PA on my way out, knowing I'd struck a nerve with Alice Baker.

CHAPTER TWENTY-TWO

There were 1,153 names, addresses, and telephone numbers on the list Charlotte Dolman had given me of men who fit the broad description I sought, spread out all over the Pacific Northwest. If I focused my queries in Multnomah and surrounding counties, that would have only shrank the field to an ample 508. My guess was that the kidnappers were local recruits; men who knew the lay of the land and could move about without arousing suspicion. Operating under that assumption, I decided to concentrate my efforts in and around Portland. That narrowed the field to 103.

I passed Pioneer Courthouse Square on the way back to the office. Clear skies, afternoon sunshine, and warm temperatures had people out and about. Smoky and Winston had camped on the northwest corner of Pioneer Courthouse Square, engaged in a serious chess match. The jazz aficionados had iced coffee and a lot of attitude. I stopped to say hello, watched the match, took and gave a few snaps, and listened to some playful banter before the call of the case forced me to move on.

After the Smoky and Winston show, I headed back to the office. I scanned the list onto our server and printed out three copies. On each copy, I highlighted the names of the men I would be investigating. I placed one copy in our paper files. The original I would file with my updated report to Destiny. The second copy I kept for myself.

Renita was in her office, working steadily away at her computer, when I returned. Her expression conveyed her intense focus. Whatever she was listening to through her wireless earbuds seemed to help maintain her concentration. She was documenting that day's case entry and barely had a smile and hello for me when I checked in with her. The first real estate firm of interviews came up empty. I filled Renita in on my day, then handed her the third copy of the men I intended to interview. Renita skimmed the list.

"And just how do you propose to interrogate all of these men?"

"Leave that to me."

"You do know that you could've highlighted these names on the PDF and printed out color copies of the list. In fact, you could've converted the PDF into a Word document and created a list of only the men you intended to interview by deleting the rest."

"I do now," I said. Actually, I did know those things. I simply found it more fun doing it my way.

Renita just shook her head, dismissing my technical ignorance as if what she had just said was commonsense for her generation. "Send me the link," she said, plugging her earbuds back in. "I'll do it later."

"Thank you," I said. She didn't hear me. Her focus was reignited. I retired to my office to mimic my partner's work ethic.

I couldn't help but swell with pride over Renita Harris. When Renita was on the beam, she was one of the best I'd ever worked with. She had come a long way from the green young woman who had walked into my office with an idealistic vision of becoming a private investigator. Renita had developed into a seasoned information specialist and an insightful and gritty interviewer. I trusted Renita not only with specific tasks involving our joint ventures, but also with cases I believed she was capable of handling on her own. Renita may not have always been on course—who is for that matter?—but she always did her best. That was all I asked of anyone. Now, if Renita could eliminate the flirt factor, we'd have a near-perfect professional team (since perfection is only a myth).

The office was quiet except for the clicking of Renita's computer keys and the steady whir of my PC fan. A fatherly grin drifted across my face as I listened to Renita plugging away before setting to work on my own list of paperwork duties.

CHAPTER TWENTY-THREE

I had considered asking Suzanne Kwong to accompany me on my interviews in the hope she could point the finger at possible suspects. My decision to forgo that idea was an easy one. It was simply too dangerous. If the guilty party were amongst those I interviewed, they would immediately realize what was going on. That could get Suzanne killed. I was going to do all I could not to allow that to happen.

One of the basic precepts behind being a good investigator is wearing out the shoe leather. Patience and single-mindedness are what is required under those conditions. I can't say it has ever been my favorite part of investigative work, but I treat it like tending a garden. You have to weed, till, and fertilize it to achieve the desired results.

"Gordon Abbott?" I said to the man standing in the doorway.

"Who wants to know?" He had a raspy voice, as if he were a long time smoker. He was a short man, wide at the shoulders, with large head and hands and stark blue eyes. His face was clean-shaven and weathered from too many unprotected days in the sun. He had on a dark blue pair of jeans that looked to be new and a Portland Speedway T-shirt that stretched across his pregnant gut.

"Jeffrey Sloan from Blue Collar America," I said, handing the man one of the fake business cards I had printed that morning. He stared at the business card as if it were alive and needed to be watched. I was wearing horn-rimmed glasses, a loose necktie, a tweed blazer, stone-washed blue jeans, and comfortable walking shoes. Gordon Sloan soaked me in. He squinted at the phony journalist ID I had dangling from around my neck.

"Have you heard of us?" I asked.

"Whatever you're selling, we ain't interested," he growled.

"Forgive me, sir, but I'm not selling anything. I'm a photographer and reporter."

Had he read the card, he would have realized that.

"So?"

"We're a new publication bent on telling the life stories of hard-working blue collar Americans who are the real backbone of this nation."

"What's that got to do with me?" Gordon leaned against the doorjamb with one thick hairy arm.

"We want to do an exclusive issue on the construction industry; specifically, construction workers. An issue dedicated to the hard-working men and women who take ideas from drawings and make them a concrete reality in our world. May I come in?"

He thought for a moment. "Why not?" he said indifferently.

I stepped inside a neat two-story bungalow filled with the mouthwatering aroma of beef stew. A short, plump woman wearing a plain sack dress and an apron decorated with farm animals stood in the middle of their living room, hurriedly wiping her damp hands on a flowered dishtowel. Mr. Abbott casually introduced himself and his wife to me. Mrs. Abbott and I graciously smiled at each other while I shook her extended hand. Mrs. Abbott had a nervous manner and twittering voice. I chalked it up as her normal reaction to meeting new people.

The television was tuned to the local news. From upstairs came voices. They sounded like two young boys in the heated throes of intense competition. *Probably playing some violent video game*, I thought as I apologized for the disturbance and explained to the Abbotts why I was there. Lydia Abbott gushed with praise over our choice of her husband as one of the people worthy of inclusion in our magazine. Gordon Abbott nodded and grinned at each compliment leveled at me by his exuberant spouse. Gordon had an arm wrapped around Lydia's round waist, basking in glowing flattery. Mrs. Abbott asked if I needed her for anything. I told her not at the moment, but I would let her know if that changed. Lydia excused herself to finish preparing dinner, asking us to "holler if we wanted anything".

Gordon Abbott sat in his easy chair, signaling for me to have a seat next to him on the sofa. After clearing it with Mr. Abbott, I placed a digital recorder on the coffee table before us and turned it on. I didn't need the recorder, but it helped seal my cover.

"Gordon—may I call you Gordon?" I said.

"Sure, my father was Mr. Abbott," Gordon said, turning down the television until it was a murmur.

"How long have you been in the construction business, Gordon?"

"About 28 years, off and on."

"Have you worked for Blue Sun the entire time?"

His eyes rolled around in his head once, like two large agates floating in a pool of milk. "About half that."

"I heard about Don Harriman," I said, making it sound like a spontaneous afterthought.

"Yeah." Gordon wiped his callused hand across his face, smoothing a grimace into a frown. "Damn shame. Don was one of the good ones."

"You were on a first name basis with Mr. Harriman?"

"Everyone was. He insisted on it."

"What do you think his wife's going to do with her husband gone? Blue Sun is a lot to handle, from what I hear."

"She'll manage, if you ask me. I wouldn't be surprised if the Ice Queen didn't have him bumped off."

"Ice Queen? She seemed nice enough when I met her," I said, making the words sound far more believable than I felt.

"The woman's all business." Gordon cocked his head to one side. "Hell, I never once seen her crack a smile."

"Lots of men are that way, too. It doesn't make them Ice Princes."

Gordon straightened his head. "You know what I mean?" Gordon said with a wink. I did, and I didn't like what he was inferring. Trying to pull a gargoyle like Gordon into a progressive mindset wasn't why I was there. My job was to find a murderer.

"Alice Harriman was with potential clients when her husband was abducted, according to the papers," I said.

"The papers also said Don was taken some place else and murdered," Gordon quickly added.

"So?"

"Who else could have arranged it? Only someone who knew Don's schedule could've pulled it off. Who better than his wife?"

According to Don Harriman's personal assistant, who I had interviewed earlier, his boss was supposed to visit two BSCS construction sites that afternoon—information Alice Baker probably had, but the kidnappers did not. Since Don Harriman wasn't expected to be at home, the kidnappers had either camped out or followed him. Someone in the neighborhood would have noticed if they had camped out. That left the latter option.

"Come on, Gordon," I said, egging him on. "From what I've heard, Mrs. Harriman built Blue Sun herself. It was already hers. Why would she need to whack her old man?"

Gordon cocked his head to one side again. "Word on the vine was Don was planning a divorce. And you know what that means in today's world?"

I'd given the divorce angle consideration. It didn't pan out. Harriman hadn't filed for divorce and had left no evidence he'd planned to leave his wife. Add to that his personal fortune, which amounted to more than forty million dollars, and that further eroded his need for greed.

"You're saying Don's wife was afraid her husband might get half of her business?"

Gordon winked. "Ain't a bad way to make a buck."

"You think Don Harriman married the owner of Blue Sun for her money?"

Gordon lowered his voice and leaned in close to me. His breath smelled of pretzels and root beer. "You've seen Alice Harriman?" he said. I nodded. "She's a hot number. She's stopped me and my boys in our tracks more than once just by walking by. So it wasn't all about the money."

"The Ice Princess," I smiled to keep him talking, "stopped you and your boys in their tracks."

"I wouldn't mind taking a crack at thawing out those pipes, if you know what I mean." Gordon leered at the thought.

"I bet your wife would."

Gordon laughed.

"Hot looks and a lot of money—what else could a man ask for?"

"How about love?"

"Love is good, don't get me wrong, but it don't pay the bills. Between you, me, and the lamp post, I think old Don was doing a little hokey pokey on the side, if you get my drift."

"You think Mrs. Harriman found out about it and had him killed?"

"I think Ms. Harriman found out about his plans for a divorce and had him killed. You didn't hear any of this from me." Gordon glanced at the recorder, suddenly looking a bit edgy. He leaned back and ran his hand across his surly mouth.

"Relax, Gordon, that's not why I'm here," I said, to reassure him. "I'm here to talk to you about you. Finding murderers is a job for the police." I gave him a consoling smile. He wasn't convinced.

"Tell you what. If at the end of this interview you believe I would do anything unethical with that recording, then I will delete it right before your eyes. Deal?" I extended my hand. Gordon smiled and shook it.

"Deal," he said in his normal speaking voice.

"Now, back to you. What current construction project are you involved in for BSCS?"

"We're building a new set of condos down in Lincoln City," Gordon answered, sounding completely at ease.

"How long have you been on that project?"

"For the last three months. Why's that important?"

"Our readers are going to want to know what you're up to. We mix in background information with current material to round out your character."

"Kind of like telling a story."

"Precisely."

"That's all right." Gordon had a satisfactory grin on his face, as if he'd just gotten the correct answer to the teacher's question.

I mixed my questions so as not to arouse suspicion to my true motives. Gordon told me his whereabouts and his personal insights into Don Harriman's murder without being aware of it. Who cared if it later dawned on Gordon what he'd done? I was there to gather information, not to make friends.

I made it clear I couldn't promise anything in terms of publication. Those things were up to the magazine editors to decide, I mentioned. For those reasons, I asked Gordon to remain quiet about the whole thing until further notice. Gordon said he understood and would do as I asked. Once I had all of the information I needed, I took Gordon's picture with Renita's digital camera and quickly and politely moved on.

And so it went with every hardhat on the list. The process of elimination was tedious. Checking out each alibi at the time of the kidnapping was also key. For most, their egos worked against them. The idea of their life stories appearing in a national magazine made them almost giddy with cooperation. For those few who were more reserved, I added a personal touch. I told the poignant story of how I'd lost my father during the construction of the Lloyd Center Mall. That, of course, never happened. My dad was alive and well in Pittsburgh, but that tale never failed to induce enough sympathy to open the less accommodating to my queries.

We were halfway to summer by the time I finished most of my interviews. Unseasonable sunshine, warm temperatures, and blue skies had become a frequent sight. The epidemic that had plagued Homicide had cooled, and Destini's caseload had lightened. Destini was ready to reclaim the Harriman case. I talked her into giving me more time. Destini agreed to two more weeks.

CHAPTER TWENTY-FOUR

Alan Slankard. His name was on the list, along with his sidekick, Tadpole. It bothered me that Al and Tadpole were lying in wait for me when I left the former Mrs. Alice Harriman. I never bought their protection story. It didn't help their creditability any that they'd tried reconstructing my anatomy. Of course, the idea had occurred to me, Destini, and Renita that Al and Tadpole could have been the kidnappers as well as the murderers if they were one and the same.

I wasn't convinced of either possibility. I believed that at the time of their attempted assault on me, they were acting under orders. I believed that because they weren't camped outside when I arrived to see Ms. Baker (a.k.a. Alice Harriman). The question was: who put them up to it? Alice Baker was the obvious suspect. If so, why would she do it? She was by no means stupid. Common sense would dictate to Alice that such a foolish move would place her under greater suspicion. Were they all in on Harriman's murder, or was there something more at stake? The pieces of the puzzle weren't adding up. I needed more to chew on.

I'd saved Al and Tadpole for last. It would have been ridiculous to attempt to fool them with my photographer/reporter scam, so I played it straight. The tricky part was getting their picture. I decided to rely on the element of surprise.

Alan Slankard lived in a porch-lined community in southeast Portland. The lawn was cut, but the hedges were overgrown. I walked up a set of plain wooden steps onto a painted wooden porch. I could hear music blaring from inside—Bruce Springsteen's 'Born in the USA'. Picture windows were on each side of the door. I couldn't see the street due to the hedges. My guess was that Slankard intentionally neglected the hedges. It meant that no one could see inside the house from the street.

I rang the doorbell and stood off to one side, hoping Slankard wouldn't decide to peek out the window I was standing in front of before answering the door. The music was turned off. I heard heavy footsteps approaching the door; felt their vibrations through the porch planks. There was a pause. I assumed Slankard was looking through the peephole. The door opened. The smell of marijuana preceded him out of the door. Slankard stepped onto the porch, turned, and looked at me. I snapped his picture.

"*Son-of-a-bitch*," Al said, squinting from the flash. "*What the hell's your problem?*"

"Just wanted to ask you a few questions about Don Harriman."

"You need a camera for that?"

"Finishing off the disk—you know how it is. Didn't anyone ever tell you how photogenic you are?"

"I'll show you photogenic when I shove that camera up your ass."

Al took an angry step toward me. I set down the camera.

"Now, now," I said, not retreating an inch. Slankard stopped in his tracks. "Let's not be hasty. We've been down that road before. This time I might not be so nice."

Slankard was wearing a shiny pair of brown leather cowboy boots, an old faded pair of blue jeans, and a puke green Led Zeppelin T-shirt that had a sweat stain in the shape of a cattle skull. Slankard still had a couple of reminders on his face from the last time we'd tangled. His hair was covered with a colorful Do Rag and his eyes were those of a man high on cannabis, dilated and foggy. Slankard slowly licked his dry lips as if pondering a philosophical dilemma.

"What the fuck do you want, Cavanaugh?" Al could have used some breath mints. I waved my hand across my face, indicating such.

"Answers to a few questions."

"About Don?"

"Yes."

"Why the hell should I tell you anything?"

"Better me than the cops."

"Why would the cops want me?"

"They might want to know why you're so reluctant to cooperate on this murder investigation. Or they may want to know why you think you should be allowed to smoke weed when the rest of us would need a doctor's prescription to light up. You do have a prescription for smoking marijuana, don't you?"

"Haven't you been keeping up? Recreational use of marijuana is legal in Oregon."

I did know that. I was hoping Al hadn't been as well informed. "That's true. But it is still subject to the same limitations as alcohol and illegal drugs."

"Meaning what?"

"You work for Blue Sun Construction Services."

"So?"

"I'm confident that company policy prohibits you from being under the influence of any substance that would hinder your performance or endanger the well-being of your fellow workers."

"What are you getting at? I'm not on the job now."

"From just smoking one joint, it can take up to ten days for the THC to process through your system."

"So?"

"Random drug testing."

"Been there, done that, passed with flying colors."

I speculated Slankard was a regular marijuana smoker in the same way some people had a couple of beers after work. If my guess was correct, there was no way he could pass a random drug test without help. The smirk on his face suggested either he had a system to cheat the RDT or enough advance warning to manage a clean bill of health.

"I know people at the Department of Labor, Al. I can have somebody swoop down on you at any time, and you would never see it coming. We both know that in the construction field, it's hard to get that drug monkey off your back once you've been saddled with it."

It was true. I could make that happen—but for ethical reasons, I wouldn't. Slankard wasn't aware of that as he was mulling over whether to call my bluff.

"Kiss my ass, Cavanaugh."

"Wrong answer."

Slankard worked his sluggish gray cells for a moment. I wasn't sure if he was still on the planet, from his expression. "What you wanna know?" he asked.

"Do you know of anyone who wanted to harm Don Harriman?"

"No."

"Do you know of any reason why anyone would have wanted to kidnap him?"

"No."

"What about his wife?"

"What about her?"

"Do you think anyone was trying to get to her through Don?"

Slankard chuckled. "No, man."

"Do you still feel that Alice Baker might be in danger?" I was holding firm to my beliefs that Slankard and Tadpole were operating under someone's orders. I was curious to see how Slankard would respond.

"No," Al said, a bit nervous and agitated. Was that a paranoid reaction from the cannabis, or had I prodded a sore spot? I filed it away.

"Was Alice Baker ever in any danger?" I asked.

Irritated, Al said, "Yes!"

"From whom?"

"Don't know; the same people who took Don. You could be in on it, for all I know." I ignored his ridiculous accusation and pressed on.

"Where were you on the day Harriman was kidnapped?"

"Working."

"Any place in particular?"

"Out in the south end of Multnomah County. We're putting up an office building over there. I'm still a part of that crew."

"Any witnesses?"

"At least three dozen, including the job foreman."

"Was Tadpole with you?"

"Tadpole—what's he got to do with this?"

"He's your friend, isn't he?"

"So what?"

"I assumed you two might be working together."

"Sometimes we do, sometimes we don't. We go where they tell us to go."

"You mean BSCS?"

"Who else?"

"Where was Tadpole working?"

Slankard grinned an evil grin; the kind that the doorman at Hell might welcome you with. "Ask him yourself."

"I intend to."

The grin disappeared. "Are we done?"

"For now."

"Then get the hell off my property."

"I'm going." I raised my hands in mock surrender before picking up Renita's camera. "One thing before I leave." I paused for effect. "When this all goes down—and it will—you're going to need all of the help you can get."

"I got nothing to hide."

"A person with nothing to hide would be more forthcoming with any information they had that might prove helpful in finding the murderer of a friend."

"You know why I won't help you, Cavanaugh?"

"Not a clue."

"Because I don't like you; not even a little. I don't talk to people I don't like."

I stepped up to Slankard. He was having a difficult time maintaining his concentration. Whatever he was smoking was powerful stuff. It made his eyelids heavy as bricks.

"If it comes out you withheld information regarding Harriman's murder, then that would mean you willfully hindered a murder investigation; and that, my friend," I poked Slankard in the sternum with my forefinger, "is a hell of a lot more serious than losing a job over smoking pot."

Slankard licked his lips in slow motion. His mouth worked open and shut a couple of times like a fish gasping for air. Without another word, Slankard went back inside his house and locked the door behind him.

Alan Slankard was lying. I was certain of that. The specifics of his deviousness were still in the gray. One thing was certain. He didn't flinch when I referred to Alice Harriman as Alice Baker. That could only mean one thing. Slankard was aware that Alice Harriman had decided to reclaim her maiden name. I doubted Alice Baker had made an overture of the fact. According to a number of construction workers I interviewed, Alice Baker was standoffish. She regarded them as little more than field hands. So how was it that a lackey like Alan Slankard could know such an intimate detail? Unless he'd heard it from the source.

I stood there for a moment, lost in my contemplation and staring at the door. Bruce Springsteen came on full bore. The music was so loud, the picture windows vibrated. I was tempted to apply a little pressure to Slankard by having Destini bring him in. Pressing charges against Al and Tadpole for assault could make that pressure happen. It probably wouldn't have worked. I couldn't see Slankard saying any more to the police than he had to me about the Harriman case. If I took Al out of circulation and it turned out he was involved, whoever else was mixed up in Harriman's death would burrow deeper than they already had. Slankard was far more valuable to me free.

CHAPTER TWENTY-FIVE

Tadpole walked to his front door. He had a noticeable limp from what I'd done to his knee. He carried a blue canvas gym bag and wore sweat socks, running shoes, a dark blue sweat suit, and a black baseball cap that read "Don't Ask Me 4 Shit" in white letters.

It was Saturday morning. Tadpole looked as though he'd come from the gym. I found that strange. If anything, I'd have thought he would avoid exercising for a bit in order not to exacerbate his injuries. Some people are diehard gym rats. Apparently, Tadpole was one of them.

I waited a few minutes just down the street from his house. Once Tadpole settled in, I slipped up the brick path to his front door, rang the doorbell, and positioned myself off to the side.

"*What the hell?*" Tadpole said after I snapped his picture. He wasn't at all happy to see me. Like his buddy, Slankard, Tadpole stepped menacingly toward me.

"How's the leg?" I asked. Tadpole stopped, looked down at his knee, and then decided to kill me with his glare instead of his hands.

"I won't be dancing anytime soon," he said in a surprisingly calm voice.

"Sorry about that." I meant it. I wasn't in the business of deliberately hurting people. That was more of his and Slankard's game.

"I'll bet you are," Tadpole said. "You got lucky."

"I do that a lot."

"Next time we rock, you'd better bring your lunch."

"I have a better idea. I'll take yours."

"You want something?"

"To talk," I said.

"The only conversation I'm interested in having is my knuckles with your face."

"Let's get past that. You try me again and you'll need crutches. Am I making myself clear?"

Tadpole's glare didn't waver; nor did his resolve. During my first encounter with Al and Tadpole, I'd assumed Slankard was the brains of the duo, the one to be most concerned about. I was wrong. If anyone had a lethal focus and dogged determination for revenge, it was Tadpole. He could kill a man with his bare hands—and probably had. It was right there in his eyes. I would need to watch my back with him.

Tadpole thought for a moment before speaking. "Like I said, what the hell do you want?"

"Answers to a few questions."

"About what?"

"Your pal, Don."

"I had nothing to do with Don's murder."

"No one said you did. I was hoping you might have some information that could steer me in the right direction."

Tadpole crossed his massive arms and stood blocking the door. "Ask your questions."

I asked Tadpole the same first two questions I'd asked Slankard, about whether he knew of anyone wanting to harm or kidnap Don Harriman. His answer was a sharp "No," to each.

"Just for the record," I said, "where were you when Don Harriman was kidnapped?"

"Working."

"Where?"

"On a Blue Sun site."

"Can anyone corroborate that?"

"Yeah, your momma; she made a lunchtime booty call."

"Anyone else besides my mother?"

"None of your goddamn business."

"I thought you liked Don Harriman," I facetiously said.

"I did. It's you I don't like."

Here we go again, I thought. "I'm still trying to find Harriman's killer, regardless of how you feel about me."

"Then look somewhere else."

Tadpole stepped back and slammed the door in my face. I let it go at that. Tadpole, like his buddy Al, wasn't going to open up about what they knew without good reason. It was up to me to find something to motivate them.

My gut told me Tadpole and Al were somehow involved in what happened to Don Harriman. What I wasn't clear on was to what extent. What would either of them have to gain from Harriman's death?

CHAPTER TWENTY-SIX

There was one person on the list I never caught up to: Barrette Wells, alias Don Harriman. I had assumed Harriman plucked the alias he used when we spoke at the community center out of thin air. When the name Barrette Wells appeared on the list I'd gotten from Alice Baker, I treated it like every other potential suspect.

No one answered each time I went to the address for Mr. Wells. I had my suspicions about what was going on. I spoke with Wells' neighbors. They were of no help. I telephoned Blue Sun job foremen all over the Portland and surrounding areas, and none of them knew Barrette Wells.

It was not surprising that no one could account for Wells. Even a drifter would garner at least a general description from passing eyewitnesses. Barrette Wells was a ghost; a creation of the late Don Harriman, but for what purpose? That was one of many unanswered questions I needed to unravel.

I coaxed the condominium manager into letting me have a look around Wells' condo. He couldn't describe Barrette Wells either. The condo manager didn't strike me as the nosy type, even if Barrette Wells did exist. One hundred bucks and my vow of silence bought me an hour.

The place was fully furnished. There were a few framed prints, cable and telephone service, and a knickknack here and there. The refrigerator, cupboards and kitchen drawers were full. There was men's clothing in one of the bedroom closets, women's clothing in the other. One bathroom contained a complete array of men's toiletries; in the other, a full complement of women's toiletries. Wells had set up shop. It was as I suspected. Don Harriman, a.k.a. Barrette Wells, used his hideaway condo for his sexual liaisons.

I put on a pair of surgical gloves and nosed around, looking for anything that might resemble a clue. The telephone, cable, and electric bills were in Barrette Wells' name. Other than that, the place was clean.

At the end of a long hall that started at the living room and went past the kitchen, both bedrooms, and a utility room was a locked door. Not one of the three keys the manager had lent me did the trick. I pulled out my little do-it-yourself entry kit and picked the lock. It wasn't standard procedure, but I doubted if anyone besides Wells would have objected.

Inside was an office with typical small office furniture, along with a printer, scanner, paper shredder, and running PC. I tried logging onto the computer without success. I couldn't crack the password. Even the text message Harriman had sent me didn't work.

On my way out, I told the manager only as much as he needed to know on how Wells' condo tied into an ongoing murder investigation. Don Harriman owned the condo, according to the manager. Harriman leased it to Barrette Wells. Any condo-related issues were always dealt with by Mr. Harriman. That information cost me another hundred and another vow of silence. So much for doing your civic duty. I saw no reason to let the condo manager in on the fact that Don Harriman and Barrette Wells were one and the same.

I left the condo manager my card in case he thought of anything else. Destini would have her people give the condo the once over, as well as have her technical experts check out the computer. I wanted Renita to have a crack at that PC before they did. A computer, peripherals, and a paper shredder didn't fit in with the rest of Harriman's love nest decorum. Why were they there?

I asked the manager if he had an extra set of keys for the condo. He did. He gave them to me after I signed a newly drawn-up agreement stating who I was and why I needed them. He was covering his butt. That condo manager was no fool.

CHAPTER TWENTY-SEVEN

There were alibis, alibis, everywhere, and not a single hole amongst them. Every possible suspect on the list was clean. Even Al and Tadpole had solid alibis for the day of the kidnapping and the estimated time of the shooting. I wasn't surprised. While I didn't believe Al and Tadpole had anything to do with Harriman's murder or kidnapping, I couldn't shake the feeling they were somehow tied to Alice Baker who, in my estimation, was at the root of this whole mess.

Renita had the same problem in regards to her queries that I had with mine. All of her possible leads were dead ends. While all of Blue Sun's competitors disliked the top dog, they also respected the real estate giant. Associates adored them because they put money in their coffers. There were a few mostly mom and pop real estate and construction operations that Blue Sun managed to run out of business. None of the defunct competitors Renita interviewed seemed too upset about it. They wrote it off as the gamble of doing business. Victims of hostile takeovers were not as forgiving. They wouldn't have minded seeing Blue Sun run out of town on a rail. Renita got the impression they were more interested in that happening in an economic rather than literal sense. I trusted my partner's instincts. We were back to square one.

CHAPTER TWENTY-EIGHT

I took Renita to Barrette Wells' condo to have her take a look at his PC. We both slipped on a pair of surgical gloves, once inside. Renita had software that allowed her to crack the computer password in a snap. Before I knew it, Renita was copying everything from Wells' PC onto a laptop she had brought with her.

While my partner worked her magic, I took another look around. Nothing had changed.

I used the bathroom with only men's toiletries when I noticed something. Both bathrooms were identical except for one thing. In the one I used, there was a silver hook with a matching back plate attached to the wall near the bathroom door. I assumed it was there for the occupant to hang their bathrobe. As in the other bathroom, there were two plastic hooks adhered to the tiles outside of the showers that could have served the very same purpose. I looked closely at the silver hook and saw nothing suspicious. A spring door came open when I pulled on it.

There was a cubbyhole fitted into the wall, just big enough to squeeze my hand inside. The hole had been cut smaller than the back plate so that the plate completely hid all evidence of it. I found a flashlight and shined it into the cubbyhole—my military intelligence training had taught me not to blindly reach for anything. After I was satisfied the cubbyhole was not booby-trapped, I reached in and extracted its contents. A turned-off smartphone and single business card with a very familiar logo was all there was. Besides the contact information, the card read: "Patrick O'Malley, Deputy Director, Portland Drug Enforcement Agency."

It was all beginning to make sense. Harriman had been playing a dangerous game. What did Harriman know that got him killed? What was Alice Baker's connection to the whole thing?

CHAPTER TWENTY-NINE

Ms. Kwong arrived at Cavanaugh Investigative Agency with a macramé shoulder bag that looked as though she'd made it herself. Suzanne had a sketchpad tucked under her arm and a large manila envelope in hand. Suzanne and I had forgotten about each other, in a sense. It had been weeks since I'd spoken to her. She had said she would stop by the office to sketch me during our one and only interview. My recent invitation to Suzanne was not to aid her in realizing her intention.

"She's attractive," Renita said with an elfin glint in her eye. "Can I trust you two alone, C. J.?" I introduced Renita to Suzanne Kwong. They shook hands. There was an instant chemistry between the two, who were sisters in humor, character, and intellect.

"Not if I have anything to say about it," Suzanne replied to Renita's question. I raised my eyebrows in surprise to Suzanne's response. Renita and Suzanne laughed.

"Which you don't, young lady," I said to Suzanne. "And don't encourage her," I added to Renita.

"We don't see a ring," Renita said, instigating Suzanne.

"That makes you fair game," Suzanne said. They were both smiling as if they had uncovered some amusing little secret about me. I didn't mention the fact that a ring hadn't stopped Suzanne in the past.

"I'm taken," I said. "Both of you need to move on."

"Just kidding, C. J.," Suzanne said. "Sort of." Suzanne and Renita laughed again.

The two of them hit it off a little too well. Their playful banter flowed free and easy, like old friends at a high school reunion. I waited for them to calm down. Suzanne looked like a casual young professional. She was wearing a peach pants suit, cream-colored blouse, and sensible brown dress shoes. Her shimmering jet-black hair was pulled back into a ponytail that sprinted to the small of her back. Touches of eyeliner, lipstick, and blush highlighted her face.

"Job interview?" I said to Suzanne.

"How'd you know?"

"Lucky guess."

"Sales clerk at an arts supply store," Suzanne said. "I just came from the interview." Suzanne set down her shoulder bag and sketchpad on the table in our waiting area on top of our neatly arranged spread of popular magazines.

"You quit Sparkling Palace," I said.

"Can you think of any reason why I shouldn't have?" Suzanne said. I shook my head. "I couldn't see going back after what happened to Don."

"What about NYU?" I said.

"That's not until the fall," Suzanne said. "Sister's gotta eat in the meantime."

"You got the job, I take it," I said.

"You know it," Suzanne said. Suzanne and Renita gave each other a high five. Their behavior was becoming nauseating.

"I've got a present for you," Suzanne said. She handed me the manila envelope. "Don originally sent this to me at Sparkling Palace. Don't ask me why. It got shuffled around the office and misplaced until it was finally mailed to me at home."

I removed the contents of the envelope. It was the diary everyone was looking for. Renita gasped. Suzanne was right. It was a cheap, black, imitation leather, paperback-sized journal that could be found at a good many stores. Pyrite-colored inlaid lettering that read "DIARY" leapt out from the cover like gaudy jewelry. A flimsy imitation leather hasp folded over the middle right of the diary like a flat, wide, supple black finger. Its surface felt like fine sandpaper. The hasp had a lock that normally required a tiny skeleton key to enter. I didn't need the key. The lock was already broken.

"Did you read it?" I asked Suzanne.

"Oh yeah," Suzanne said with a lascivious grin and a knowing nod. "There's some wild stuff in that black book. Including some details of me and Don's sordid little love jousts."

"I can't wait to check it out," Renita said, grinning. Suzanne gave Renita a sideways glance. Renita realized her mistake. Renita put an arm around Suzanne as if she were consoling a troubled friend.

"I meant that in a strictly professional sense," Renita said, "in terms of how it could have a positive effect on the Harriman investigation."

"I understand," Suzanne said. Neither of us bought Renita's endeavor to smooth over her faux pas. Suzanne appeared amused by her attempt. Renita dropped her arm from Suzanne's shoulders. An awkward moment was in place.

"Did you break the lock?" I asked Suzanne.

"I did," she answered without any misgivings.

What Suzanne didn't realize was she had tampered with probable evidence involved in an ongoing murder investigation; an offense punishable by law. Destini came to mind. I doubted Destini would have cared about Suzanne reading the diary. Destini would have probably lectured Suzanne on the serious consequences of her actions and let it go at that. I passed on the lecture. Instead, I decided to employ the former military decree regarding gays in the armed services, "Don't ask, don't tell."

"Anything worth dying for in here?" I asked. I held the diary before me like a priest attempting to use it to ward off evil spirits.

"Depends on who reads it," Suzanne said. "In my opinion, no. If you're Alice Harriman, that's a whole other story."

I let the diary come to rest in my right hand at my right hip. "Does Alice Baker know you have Don's diary?"

"Alice who?" Suzanne said.

"Alice Harriman," I said. "She's taken back her maiden name of Baker."

"Not to my knowledge. I certainly haven't told her."

"Keep it that way," I said. "There's no reason for you to be involved in this any more than necessary." Renita glanced quizzically at me. Renita sensed my concern for Suzanne's safety and chimed in.

"C. J. and I can handle it from here," Renita said.

"Thanks for dropping it by, Suzanne," I said. "Did Harriman ever take you to a condo for one of your rendezvous?"

"A couple of times."

"Why didn't you mention that before?" I asked.

"It probably slipped my mind. Guess I was more dazed by Don's death than I realized."

"That's understandable," Renita said.

"Do you remember anything unique about your time with Don at the condo?" I asked.

"Unique?" Suzanne said.

"Different from the norm," Renita said.

"Besides the sex?" Suzanne said.

"Yes," I said.

Suzanne thought for a long moment. "Nope."

"Did you ever see Harriman on his computer?" I asked.

"Computer," Suzanne said. "What computer?" Suzanne looked confused. *Harriman must have kept that room locked*, I thought. I moved on.

"What about people or actions?" I said. "Did you encounter anyone else, or did Harriman do anything that might seem odd while in your company?"

"People, definitely not. We were always alone and were never disturbed. Any odd actions—let me think." Suzanne did just that. "Don did disguise himself both entering and leaving the condo. He wore this short brunette wig, dark sunglasses, and a Mariner's baseball cap. That was the only time he ever bothered—disguising himself, that is."

Renita and I looked at each other. We were both thinking the same thing. Harriman used that condo for something more than gettin' busy; that much we'd already established. The fact that Harriman disguised himself confirmed a few of our other suspicions. Suzanne not knowing about the office, or the real reason Harriman wore a disguise, proved she knew nothing about Barrette Wells or Harriman's possible DEA connection.

"Anything else?" I said to Suzanne.

"No," Suzanne said. "We'd have sex. Before we left the condo, we'd shower in separate bathrooms, dress in separate bedrooms, and then Don would take me home or drop me wherever I wanted to go."

"Why the separate bedrooms and bathrooms?" Renita asked.

"To lessen the chance of making a mistake," I answered. They both stared at me. "It was pretty obvious," I continued. "With separate cleaning and dressing areas, there was less chance of Harriman bringing home a clue to his wife that he was fooling around."

"Answer me this, C. J.," Suzanne said. "What did Don do, the times we didn't have sex at his condo?"

"He still showered at the condo," I said. "The only time he didn't was when you two had sex at his home. Then he used the guest bathroom."

Suzanne looked astonished. "You're right. We did use the guest bathroom."

"Did you ever have sex in his wife's bed?" I said to Suzanne, already knowing the answer.

Suzanne thought for a moment. "Never."

"He was still taking a chance, having sex in their home," Renita said.

"Not as big a chance as you might think," I said. "Suzanne was their house cleaner. I'm willing to bet she's the only one Harriman had sex with in his house. So things like the smell of her perfume, or an earring or a piece of jewelry accidentally being left behind, could be easily explained. As long as nothing incriminating was ever found on his person, he was home free— no pun intended. Harriman was an old-time player who knew the game of infidelity well."

"What about the diary?" Renita said.

"Yeah," Suzanne said. "Don kept it in his desk in the study at their home, right under his wife's nose."

"You saw it?" I said.

"With my own two eyes," Suzanne said. "It's the one you're holding in your hand."

I held up the diary. "This same diary you can get at a dozen different stores."

"What are you getting at, C. J.?" Renita said.

"Did you ever see what was in the diary Harriman showed you, Suzanne?"

Suzanne thought for a moment. "Nooo," she said, drawing out the word.

"For all you know, there could've been nothing written in it."

"But why would he do something like that?" Renita said.

"To assure Suzanne's affections for as long as he wanted," I said. "I wouldn't have been surprised if Harriman hadn't planned on destroying the blank diary right before your eyes, giving you some heart-wrenching, shame-ridden soliloquy about how he had to break it off with you and return to his beloved wife."

Renita said, "But what about the fact that Harriman was—"

"Fooling around with so many women?" I said. "Who knows?"

I deliberately cut Renita off. With a quick cut of my eyes from Renita to Suzanne and back, Renita realized why. Renita was about to announce that Harriman may have been involved with the DEA; speculation that I didn't want Suzanne privy to. The less Suzanne knew, the less likely any of the dangerous players would come looking for her.

"What an asshole!" Suzanne said. "And to think I felt sorry for him."

"You were only in it for the sex, remember?" I said.

"That still doesn't mean he wasn't a jerk," Suzanne said.

"Why keep a diary at all?" Renita said.

"Who knows?" I said. "The man was a player. Could be he was trying out a new twist. Perhaps he got a kick out of keeping track of his conquests. Or maybe he simply wanted to have something to look back on before the days of Viagra set in."

"He couldn't simply video record like everyone else?" Renita said.

"Too risky," I said. "A diary could be disputed; written off as pure fantasy if Harriman could get all other parties involved to corroborate. When you have money, that's always a viable option."

"And how do you know all of this, C. J.?" Renita said. They both stood akimbo, awaiting my explanation.

"I'm an investigator," I nonchalantly said. "It's my job to figure these things out."

"I'm an investigator, too," Renita said. "And all of that speculation went right by me."

"That's why you're my junior partner. By the time you become a full partner, that won't happen. Now, can we focus on what's important here?"

"Um-hum," they said in unison.

Innuendoes and insinuations are two gifts women develop far better than men do. When a woman wants a man to feel guilty, the truth is irrelevant. You will search your conscience to justify her suspicions. Two or more women applying guilt pressure, and all you can do was ride the wave to its end and hope you can recover from the wipeout. I needed to change the subject.

"Are those digital mug shots ready, Renita?" I asked.

"Yes," Renita said, raising an eyebrow to let me know she knew exactly what I was doing. "It's all set up on the network."

"Have Suzanne take a look at them," I said. "Maybe she can pick out the kidnappers."

Suzanne looked puzzled. What I did compile from burning the shoe leather was digital photographs of each of the men I'd interviewed. With Renita working her computer magic, we were able to fit the photos with black cyber ski masks to show Suzanne Kwong in the hope that she could identify one or both of the kidnappers from them. It was a long shot, but it was all we had to go on.

"I'll explain," Renita said to Suzanne. "Right this way." Renita gestured the way to her office with a graceful wave of her arm.

"Aren't you forgetting something?" Suzanne asked me as Renita attempted to lead her away.

I stared quizzically at Suzanne. "What?" I said; but I hadn't forgotten. She and Renita weren't the only ones who could be coy. Suzanne picked up her shoulder bag and sketchpad. I acknowledged her inference with a slight grin.

"Right," I said. "Why don't you sketch Renita after you've had a look at those mug shots? You'd love to have a sketch of yourself, wouldn't you, Renita?"

"Sure," Renita said matter-of-factly.

"I'll be glad to," Suzanne said, "as soon as we're done. It'll just take a moment. You'll see."

Suzanne grabbed my arm and ushered me into my office. Renita followed, stopping at the doorway.

"Act natural," Suzanne said, after seating me behind my desk. She removed a handful of sharp pencils from her handbag and laid them on my desk in front of her. After taking a moment to equally space her pencils, Suzanne opened her sketchpad, then sat erect across the desk from me.

"While you're tied up, C. J., why don't I get started on the Harriman diary?" Renita said, leaning against the doorframe.

"This won't take long," Suzanne said. "Now look toward your computer screen."

I did as the artist instructed.

"Too far," Suzanne said. "Angle back toward me. Better. . .better. . .perfect! Hold it right there." I stared over Suzanne's right shoulder, looking at the framed print of Jacob Lawrence's "The Builders" on my wall.

"I thought you wanted me to act natural," I said.

"For a sketch, this *is* natural," Suzanne said. "Now be still. It'll be over before you know it."

"That's what my dentist says," I said. "And he's always wrong."

"Then you need to change dentists," Suzanne said. "Now, hold still. I can promise you that this will be painless."

"Mind if I breathe?" I said.

"Only if you have to," Suzanne sarcastically said.

Renita was thoroughly amused. I could see Renita making faces at me out of the corner of my eyes. I tried not feeling like an idiot. My eyes kept gravitating down toward the diary that was under my right hand.

"There," Suzanne said with a flourish. "All done." It had taken her less than fifteen minutes. Renita was impressed. I could tell by the look in her eyes as she took in the sketch. I had to admit: so was I, when I saw it.

"You are good, Suzanne," Renita said.

"NYU will be lucky to have you," I said to Suzanne.

"Thanks," Suzanne said. She was beaming.

"Can I keep it?" I said. I wanted to show it to Destini.

"*No way*," Suzanne said. "This one's going in my collection. I can do another if you're willing to sit again."

"Next time," I said.

"Draw me next," Renita said.

"Before you do," I said, "have Suzanne look at those mug shots."

"Will do," Renita said.

The ladies went into Renita's office. I closed my door and dove into Harriman's diary.

CHAPTER THIRTY

Suzanne came up empty on the digital mug shots. The generic ski masks Renita used were incorrect. Suzanne dove in and altered the eyeholes, mouth hole, and texture of the mask to precisely match those of her would-be assailants, teaching Renita a trick or two about computer graphics in the process.

We gathered in the waiting area when they were done. I asked Suzanne if she had a problem appearing in Harriman's diary.

"No," she said. "I didn't like the way he depicted some of our—to put it delicately—trysts. At times, Don was poetic in his descriptions and comments. Other times, he made bottom feeders proud. And then some of it was just plain space cadet weird."

Renita and I gave an empathetic nod to her response.

"May I see the sketch you made of Renita?" I asked Suzanne. Like mine, her sketch captured not only Renita's physical features, but also her essence.

"She looks better than I do," I said feigning irritation.

"C. J., the artist can only recreate what the subject brings to the table," Renita said playing along. "She's not a miracle worker."

"Stop it, you two," Suzanne said, refusing to chime in. "You both look great, whatever that means. Art is not a competition; it's an individual expression—a reflection of our unique view of our world manifested through the aesthetic prisms of our human senses."

Renita and I were both stunned at her declaration. I was impressed and proud of her stance. Suzanne may have been flippant about a number of matters in her life, but art clearly was not one of them.

"Alright, Professor Kwong," Renita said. Renita gave Suzanne a high five. I had to give Suzanne some as well, for her eloquent definition.

"Thanks for coming in, Suzanne," I said. "We'll let you know if there's anything else."

"Let's do lunch," Renita said to Suzanne, exhibiting the type of enthusiasm old friends muster when they really want to stay in touch.

"Works for me," Suzanne reciprocated. "I'm busy the rest of the week. Next week some time?"

"It's a date," Renita said. "Call or text me when and where."

"Will do. I have your cell."

When did they exchange cell numbers? I thought. *I am so out of the loop.*

Renita walked Suzanne to the elevators, the two of them behaving like teenage besties. I returned to my office and picked up where I left off in Don Harriman's diary.

Harriman's diary was no more than a self-indulgent explicit manifest of his sexual conquests and perversions over the last year. Suzanne was right. If anyone would have been incensed by its contents—aside from the people appearing in it—Alice Baker would be the one. Harriman had two lovers in Multnomah County besides Suzanne Kwong, and three others in western Washington. There was no mention of a DEA connection.

Before Renita read it, I assigned her the tedious task of scanning and photocopying the diary. One copy was for myself. One copy was for Renita. The third copy was for our hard copy files. The original I would give to Destini, following my next report. The scanned copy would be loaded onto our network.

Of the six women written about in detail in Harriman's diary, I was aware of three: Suzanne Kwong, Harriman's neighbor Janice Bigelow, and Alice Baker's PA Charlotte Dolman. Of those three women, only Charlotte Dolman was married. Did that suggest a possible motive for Mrs. Dolman, perhaps? If Mrs. Dolman knew the diary existed, she might have regarded it as being both humiliating and a viable threat to her marriage. There was only one way to find out.

I fired off an email, with my official report attached, to Destini, informing her of the diary's existence but deliberately omitting my finding the hidden smartphone and DEA card until I could follow up on its significance. Destini telephoned less than half an hour later. We agreed to meet for lunch at Pazzo Ristorante just around the corner from my office. Destini stressed that I not forget the diary.

CHAPTER THIRTY-ONE

It had been six days since I'd last seen the love of my life. That had been far too long. Life in Homicide had returned to normal. Destini had gone from being overwhelmed to simply too busy. Due to our prolonged absence from each other, we momentarily set aside our usual professional decorum. We kissed, hugged, and complimented one another on our appearances. I seated Destini, made myself comfortable, and then we got down to business.

"I read your report," Destini said. "Interesting stuff."

"If you thought my report was interesting, wait until you read Harriman's diary."

I handed Destini the black book with the broken lock. Destini glanced at it briefly before stuffing the diary into her shoulder bag. The question of whether or not the diary remained police property or was to be turned over to Alice Baker was no longer my headache. That had become a matter between Baker's attorney and the Portland Police Bureau.

"Did your people have a chance to go over Don Harriman's (a.k.a. Barrette Wells') condo?" I asked.

"No."

"Good, that'll give you a chance to read the diary. Garner a sense of the condo's hedonist history. You'll have a better feel for the place once you do."

"I'll bet."

I smiled. Destini smiled back. And then, as if we were two children being scolded about the evils of finding humor in such a macabre incident, our smiles dissolved, replaced with the deadpan expressions of investigators at work.

"Our victim was a busy man," Destini said. "What's your take on all of this?"

"I still believe there was something other than infidelity behind Harriman's murder."

"Do you have any proof?"

"No."

"Any solid leads to the contrary?"

"No."

"Then we go with what we have."

For the first time since the Harriman case broke, others besides Alice Baker had possible grounds to murder Don Harriman. Destini insisted, and I concurred, that the irate lover—or wives'—incentives be followed up. For the moment, that made infidelity the primary motive behind the crime. Infidelity not limited to Alice Baker. It was not unheard of for a spouse, upon discovering they had been cheated on, to become enraged enough to kill. The bigger question became: who, of the six women mentioned in the diary, was capable of murder?

"Irate spouses or lovers don't have the objects of their disdain kidnapped," I said. "Revenge is usually exacted swiftly and violently with no forethought or reasoning involved."

"True; we don't know who pulled the trigger. And don't forget: nobody but Suzanne Kwong saw the kidnappers."

"No one could make up the story she did."

"Unless she was properly motivated."

That thought had crossed my mind. "You're suggesting Suzanne Kwong may have been involved in this whole thing from the start," I said.

"Could be."

"What's her motivation?"

"You tell me."

"It doesn't pan out. Suzanne brought attention to the scheme. Without her, there would be no eyewitness linking us to the eventual murder of Don Harriman."

"Touché," Destini said in regards to my point about the possible murder link. "Assuming the alleged kidnappers were involved in the killing."

"Let's assume they weren't. Then what?"

"From what you've told me, C. J., all roads of conjecture lead back to the widow, or one of the people in Harriman's diary." Destini paused for a minute to wipe some red spaghetti sauce from her chin with her white cloth napkin. "Maybe I should bring in Alice Harriman—I mean Baker—for questioning," Destini said.

"Do me a favor and don't."

"Reason?"

"Bringing her in might scare away any potential ground-breaking clues if she's involved."

"Bringing her in might dislodge them."

"You've met Alice Baker."

"I've met Alice Harriman."

"Do you think either one would talk?"

Destini thought for a moment. "I see your point. What about blackmail; any possibilities there?"

"If the diary is true—which by all accounts, so far, seems to be the case—then Don Harriman is unquestionably a womanizer," I said. "What could he gain from becoming a blackmailer? He didn't need money, so that angle didn't figure. Emotional or sexual blackmail—not in Ms. Kwong's case."

"What about attempting to gain control over someone, or excavating vital information?"

"What sort of vital information?"

"Inside information on the real estate markets, for example."

"None of his conquests had those types of connections."

"Maybe he had another angle."

"Not likely. The type of control you're referring to, Harriman already had, according to his diary. I don't believe any of his conquests had access to top secret government information."

Destini smirked. "I gather you're right on the money, there. All the same, I'm going to keep an eye on Ms. Baker. Make sure she doesn't have any plans to skip town."

"Understood. Renita and I will stay on top of things. We'll know more after we've interviewed the other women mentioned in the diary."

"How is that nitwit partner of yours?" Destini said with a grin. I looked at Destini for a moment. She was trying to get a rise out of me. *That's not going to work today, honey,* is what I thought.

"Fine, and she's not a nitwit," is what I said.

"Tell her I said hi." Destini smiled a phony smile, like one of those rehearsed, empty grins you get from waiters and cashiers in so many establishments these days.

"Will do." I allowed the moment to pass while I chewed my scampi.

We continued our lunch, discussing more of the Harriman case as well as some of Destini's other cases, with a touch of our personal lives thrown in. Destini was pleased with our handling of the murder investigation, although she never once mentioned Renita by name. Her higher-ups didn't complain. They knew my rep. Renita and I were making steady progress and were working pro bono. Still, I could sense the Harriman case was an intriguing puzzle to Destini. While Destini agreed to grant us more time, she was itching to reclaim the Harriman case for herself.

CHAPTER THIRTY-TWO

After Renita had a crack at the diary, we sat down and discussed how to proceed. Harriman made it clear in his diary he chose women to have affairs with based on their ability to understand that it was just a fling. He had no intention of leaving Alice. Believe it or not, according to his diary, he loved her too much. He blamed his unfaithful nature on his inability to control his sexual cravings for—as he put it—foreign flesh. He needed variety. No one woman could ever quench the lust that burned in him. Renita and I both agreed that was a bunch of bull, although we did concede he might have been a sex addict.

I had filled Renita in on the discussion I'd had with Destini on the previous afternoon regarding the diary and its implications for the case. When I told Renita, Destini had said hi, Renita snorted. "Are you certain it wasn't 'die, bitch?'" Renita said. I let it drop, moving the conversation back to our case.

We only had a threadbare circumstantial motive for murder. Alice Baker, knowing of her husband's cheating ways, had yet to be proof enough that infidelity had been the cause behind Harriman's death.

It didn't matter what my gut was telling me about the Harriman case. Renita and I needed to weed out all possible motives for murder. Harriman's diary pointed at six potential suspects—seven, if Alice Baker knew of its contents. Renita and I agreed to approach the diary suspects from three directions: anger over the breakup, jealousy, or fear of exposure. A little preliminary foraging revealed to us that two of the three Western Washington women were married.

We flipped a coin. Renita lost. I chose the three women in Multnomah County to interview and re-interview. I gave Renita the option of whether to interview the western Washington women in person or by phone. Renita opted to do it in person. I agreed with her decision. By phone, a person can be evasive; even cut you off. The phone also serves as an early warning system to alert your interviewee about what's going on, giving them a chance to ready their defenses and bolster their guard. Surprising them in person can work like a Muhammad Ali jab. If they saw it at all, it was usually after they'd been hit with it.

***

"Two days tops," I told Renita, and I wanted itemized expense reports. "This isn't a vacation," I stressed. Renita said she understood. I believed her. Renita would leave first thing Monday morning. That would give her the weekend to practice her lines. I literally wrote a script for Renita to follow in order to get the three western Washington women she would interview to talk.

"Hello, Mrs. or Ms. [name goes here]. My name is Renita Harris and I work for the Cavanaugh Investigation Agency. I was wondering if I could have a word with you regarding your affair with Don Harriman? You see, he kept a diary of the when and where as well as some of the graphic depictions of your sexual liaisons. My presence here is not intended to embarrass or spotlight your supposed affair. I'm only hoping you can answer a few simple questions that may help us nail Don Harriman's murderer. I can promise that if you answer these questions, you won't be bothered by me again. Not only that, but I'll do everything in my power to make certain that your affair with Don Harriman remains a secret."

If it flew, great; at the very least, the script would help keep Renita on point. Renita could take it from there. Her instincts and experience could guide her the rest of the way. If it didn't, Renita would need to apply a little pressure by suggesting that she could not help but involve the police because of the necessity of having a few vital questions answered. That would not be a bluff. Even if they answered the questions, neither Renita nor myself could guarantee the DA would not find it necessary to air their dirty laundry. Of course, Renita wouldn't mention that prospect.

I was about to shut down my office PC for the weekend when an email arrived from the Portland Fire Marshall. Their crime lab had found chemical traces in some of the basement wood samples that appeared to have been previously burned. MDP-2-P, nickel, and methylamine were three of the chemicals the arson drug lab was able to isolate—ingredients used in the concoction of 3,4-methylenedioxymethamphetamine, commonly known as MDMA, Ecstasy, XTC, E, M, X, Adam, or bean and roll; one of the illicit synthetic drugs currently sold at nightclubs and Raves. Just because I was no longer DEA didn't mean I didn't keep up. The picture became clear. Derek Knopp had been running a drug lab out of his home.

According to the Fire Marshall, the scenario went as follows: Knopp had an earlier accident while cooking his product; one that resulted in a severe chemical fire. In an attempt to cover his mishap, Knopp started a gasoline fire.

I concurred with the Fire Marshall's reasoning regarding the fires, albeit they were not very bright of Knopp. He was a chemist. He should have known the second fire would not mask the truth. My only guess regarding Knopp's actions was that he became so frightened of being discovered, he panicked. Torching the house was a quick gamble that not only didn't pay off, but also cost Knopp his life.

The Knopp case was officially sealed. The Fire Marshall had signed off on it. The criminal investigation division of arson control was satisfied. Once I filed my final report with Carl Wheaton regarding the Knopp house fire, Lunsford Insurance would be content. Derek Knopp was running a drug lab and literally got burned in the process. I had no sympathy for Knopp. How many lives had he maimed or taken due to his chemical creations before his number was called? All of the evidence pointed a big fat red arrow toward the bull's eye reading 'case closed.'

Then why were my knuckles tingling?

CHAPTER THIRTY-THREE

The weekend belonged to me. Bright and early Saturday morning, I ran six miles and spent quality time with my zebra finches Toussaint, Coretta, Claude, and Truth; as well as my tropical fish. I did laundry before going to the community center to counsel teenagers on whatever they brought to the table. The afternoon found me losing more outdoor pick-up basketball games than winning. Evening found my twin terriers, Booker and Andrew, and I spending leisure time at local Laurelhurst Park. That night brought with it a surprise visit from Destini, who was nude beneath one of my borrowed sweatshirts, which fit her like a sweater dress. Accompanying her was a bottle of merlot and the sensuous promise of passion without the slightest hint of shoptalk.

I cleaned house on Sunday. My roses needed tending, as did my backyard flower garden. The afternoon sky was a misty blue. A bright yellow sun beamed on a sedentary world. I serenely gardened beneath its glaring eye and tangy kisses. The twins played, watched me garden, explored, ate, drank, sunned, then played some more. It was, by all accounts, a blissful weekend; a welcomed respite.

It was the last peace I would experience for some time to come.

CHAPTER THIRTY-FOUR

It was Renita. She had called the office at 9:04 a.m. to inform me that she had arrived safely in Seattle and to give me her room number, per my request. Her room overlooked Elliot Bay. I knew this because Renita gloated on the topic for at least a minute. Renita also reported that the waterfront was more crowded than usual. Seafair, the largest community festival of its kind in the Pacific Northwest, was in full swing, bringing thousands of visitors into the area from all over the world. Being that as it may, Renita never made the connection that I had to pull some strings to get her a quality hotel room with just such a view. I gave Renita a stern reminder of why she was in Seattle. She laughed.

"Don't worry, C. J., I know why I'm here," Renita said after her laugh died.

"Do you remember your lines?"

"What sort of question is that?"

"A direct one."

"Of course I remember. A grade school child could remember those few simple lines."

"Let's hear them."

"You're kidding. You want me to audition?"

"The word is 'rehearse'. Who do you plan to interview first?"

"Shirley Faber. She lives furthest out, in Bellingham. Then I plan to interview Melanie Collins in Ballard, and finally, Jennifer Norton in Queen Anne."

"I'm Shirley Faber. I've just answered the door. May I help you? I say if I'm in a good mood. Now let's hear your rap."

Renita sighed. After a beat, Renita recited her lines flawlessly, having added a few personal touches that helped make it even more convincing.

"Oh yeah, you're ready," I said, impressed by the sincerity Renita exuded in delivering her lines.

"This I know."

"Need anything from me?"

"You waiting in my bed in nothing but your boxers when I return from my rounds would be nice."

Whoa, I didn't see that coming, I thought.

"Talk to you when you get back," I said, brushing Renita off.

Renita laughed. "I take that to mean you'll think about it."

"Did you get anything from Wells' computer files?"

"Nice change of pace. Everything I downloaded, I loaded onto our network. Each file has its own password, so it's slow going. On top of that, some of the files are encrypted. So far, I've only been able to bank a few passwords. Those files were simply general information about Blue Sun; nothing special. Whatever Harriman was hiding must have been serious, to go through all of this trouble."

"Make getting at those files Priority One, when you get back."

"You're welcome to have a crack at them, C. J."

"Right. I'd be slower than Moses crossing the desert. What about that message Harriman sent me; anything on that?"

"Not yet."

"It has to mean something. With death knocking at your door, you don't waste time sending false clues."

"Agreed," Renita said. "Now, back to our previous topic of conversation. You have your choice of boxers, briefs, or nothing at all."

"Good luck, Renita," I said, continuing to ignore her advances. "If you run into trouble or need anything pertinent to the case, I'll be here."

"I can handle it." I could hear the smile in her voice. "But thanks all the same, C. J."

When we were done, I locked up the office, jumped in my car, and made my way over to west Portland to have a little chat with the first of my interviews for the day.

CHAPTER THIRTY-FIVE

Charlotte Dolman consented to meet me at Fernhill Park on the northeast side of Portland. I had prodded her into such a meeting by mentioning her affair with Don Harriman. In order to keep a lid on things, Mrs. Dolman needed to maintain as much distance as she could between herself and the investigating authorities of Don Harriman's murder. I purposed that was doable, gathering she'd told me everything she knew about anything involving the case.

Mrs. Dolman was waiting for me when I arrived. Charlotte had chosen an inconspicuous spot near high bushes and deciduous trees that formed a dense natural wall at the farthest end of the park. The morning was bright and comfortable. I casually approached Mrs. Dolman, looking around to make certain nothing was amiss. When murder is involved, you can't be too cautious. Everything looked and felt calm.

Charlotte wore dark blue jeans, tennis shoes—no socks—a light sweater, a blue baseball cap, and large mirrored sunglasses. Her dark, shiny ponytail was looped through the back of her Portland Beavers baseball cap. Her skin was pale; her lips their natural pink. I couldn't see her eyes; but if what I could see of her face was any indication, she wasn't wearing any eye makeup. She sat with her legs crossed and her arms folded tight across her chest. She looked like a pissed-off soccer mom. I couldn't say I blamed her.

I sat next to Charlotte on the park bench, politely nodded, smiled, and then took one last look around. The moment reminded me of my undercover days, a time in my life I did not miss.

"Ask your questions and make it fast," Charlotte snapped. "I've got to meet my family in Beaverton in an hour."

"Let's blow by the affair between you and Harriman and get to some of the other details," I said. "What do you remember about Don Harriman's behavior that could be viewed as out of the ordinary?"

"Nothing."

"Come on, you're not even trying. Did he behave oddly at any time? Ask any strange questions?"

Charlotte thought for a moment. Her face was taut. Her lips puckered and then relaxed. She was making a sincere effort; I'd give her that much. Especially considering that she would have liked nothing better than to see me on a slab at the morgue at that moment.

"There was one thing," Charlotte said; then stopped. A few moments passed and nothing was forthcoming. Her silence was deliberate. Charlotte was trying to get under my skin, her passive-aggressive way of needling me. Under less serious circumstances, I would've toyed with Charlotte Dolman. But I had no time for bullshit. I needed answers.

"Cut the suspense," I said. "I thought you were in a hurry, so let's stop playing games."

My tone startled her. Charlotte went right into the rest of her answer. "Don asked about blueprints for the houses we'd been building," she began apprehensively. "It seemed some of them had construction done that wasn't showing up on the original designs. The recent house fire involving that chemist—what's his name?"

"Derek Knopp," I said.

"That's him. It's one of ours, so Blue Sun is rebuilding his house. Don got a call from his construction foreman that the old plans were incomplete. Don went to the site to check it out and discovered a whole section had been added to the house that never appeared on the original plans."

"I'm sure that happens all of the time."

"Yes, it does. Don became interested because it was going to cost more to rebuild the house than he had estimated from the original plans."

"Harriman was looking for a way to cut corners."

"That's why Don went rooting around for information on the new construction..."

"Let me guess: he couldn't find any."

"No quotes, no permits, no plans, no nothing. As far as the city of Portland was concerned, the new construction never happened. It's rare there's no paper trail of any kind."

"What does that tell you?" I asked, masking my own suspicions.

"If I were to say—which I'm not—it smells like under-the-table dealings."

I nodded. "Why?"

"More profit, why else?"

"I suppose that sort of thing goes on all of the time in the construction business."

"Not at Blue Sun."

I stared at Charlotte Dolman. She stared back. I believed she was telling the truth about both Don Harriman and Blue Sun, although it would've been more convincing if I could have seen her eyes.

"There's more, isn't there?" I said.

"You're not so dumb after all." Charlotte had gotten her cockiness back. I needed to keep her aware of who was holding the reins.

"Smart enough to know not to insult someone who can turn your life into a Jerry Springer episode with one phone call," I said.

Her attitude cooled a little. "Don started looking into other homes that might have had construction done without his knowledge," Charlotte said. "I think at first it was more about his ego being bruised than anything else. Something like that big-ticket construction oversight happening on his watch. But then something else crept in. Something I couldn't quite put my finger on."

"Did Harriman say what he was up to?"

"No. When I asked Don about it, he claimed he was past that one little incident. I could tell he was lying. Do you think that what Don was looking into might have something to do with his death?"

"Could be."

"You can't believe Alice Baker had anything to do with Don's murder. I mean, she's tough; but I can't see her killing anybody. Especially Don. She was crazy about that guy."

"What about you? How'd you'd feel about Don?"

"He was sexy and exciting while it lasted, but I knew it was just a fling."

"Let me ask you something. It's none of my business and I won't hold it against you if you refuse to answer."

Charlotte prudently waited.

"Weren't you the least bit concerned that you were sleeping with your boss's husband?"

"That's what made it exciting: being in another women's nest right under her nose."

It was just another installment in my swelling encyclopedia of 'Why I'll Never Understand Women' which I mentally filed away.

"If you say so," I said. "Thanks for your help."

Charlotte Dolman got up and scurried away. I watched her speed off in her forest-green SUV, wondering how many more women in the world were seeking that same sexual thrill. I thought of Destiny. Did she harbor those same fantasies? How many of them didn't involve me?

I had mentally gotten off track. There were some facts in evidence to the case that I needed to bring into the light. Don Harriman was on to something. Whatever it was, had it cost him his life? Or was this simply a case of infidelity leading to murder, as Destini suggested? I wasn't going to find the answers sitting on a park bench enjoying the sun. There were two more interviews I still needed to conduct. What Charlotte Dolman had told me played no part in them. The real killer may have already known what Harriman was up to. Destiny and Renita would hear about these new developments. I had my own suspicions as to where they led.

CHAPTER THIRTY-SIX

"Mr. Cavanaugh."

Despite her warm smile and gracious greeting, Janice Bigelow was neither surprised nor pleased to see me. Her expressive dark brown eyes told me so. I was guessing that someone had informed her about the diary prior to my coming. The question was, who? It was certainly no one from my office. Destini would have notified me if she'd planned to talk to anyone regarding the diary. I was also confident that Destini had respected my wishes to grant me more time before she told Alice Baker about it, too. That left Charlotte Dolman, Suzanne Kwong, or one of the women Renita was interviewing in western Washington. I decided to sit on my suspicions and keep Janice Bigelow in the dark that I suspected anything.

Janice politely stepped aside and ushered me into her home. I accepted her offer to sit, making myself comfortable on the same spot on her country-style sofa as I had the last time I visited. Janice got us tea and shortbread cookies. She remembered. The chamomile tea was sweetened just the way I liked it. It tasted even better than the last time I paid her a visit. After a few minutes of small talk, we got down to business.

"Don Harriman mentioned you in his diary."

Her head lowered. With it, so did her spirit. Her reaction seemed deep-rooted and genuine. I carefully watched Janice Bigelow, despite her apparent sincerity—if for no other reason than to keep my wits sharp.

"I didn't know he kept a diary. If I had, maybe—," she sighed. "I don't know. It all happened so fast. Don was one of my regular customers. He had been since I started the business. We would always flirt and tease one another before; but never anything serious. Then one day, a few months before he was killed, Don stopped by to pick up his order. We were toying with each other, until the next thing I know, he kissed me. Before I knew it, I was kissing him back. One thing led to another and we wound up in my bed together. God, I don't know how I'm going to face Alice when she finds out."

If she doesn't already know, I thought. *Perhaps Alice Baker was the one who told you about the existence of the diary.* "From what I read in the diary, the first time sounded like a spontaneous moment."

Janice lifted her head, but not her spirit. "It was," she said with false exuberance. "That's exactly what it was!"

"What led to the second and third and so on?"

"It was so easy, with Don living right next door," Janice said, her exuberance gone. "I couldn't say I didn't find Don attractive. I'm not seeing anyone, and you know what they say: having someone else's man is better than no man at all."

Another philosophical addition to the encyclopedia, I thought. "I didn't know they said that."

"Well, they do."

"The two of you met here for your rendezvous?"

"Yes."

"How'd Harriman slip in without any of the neighbors noticing?"

"We have a common path that connects our backyards. Don always used that, using picking up his orders as a front. I suppose if I were a smart business woman, I would have sold him more of my products that way."

Her smile was faint. I felt sorry for Janice Bigelow. She was the first person I'd spoken to who seemed genuinely remorseful about having had an affair with Don Harriman.

"Janice, I'm not here to judge you. My purpose is the same as my first visit; and that's to find Harriman's murderer."

My sentiments were sincere. What I hadn't forgotten was that Janice had somehow found out about the diary before I arrived. I jostled with the idea of confronting her about the leak. There were too many unanswered questions surrounding this case. Pressing her on the matter could make matters worse, making a tough investigation even tougher.

Janice breathed deep. Her shoulders rose and dropped with her breath. "I'm all for that." She sounded relieved.

"Good. Then what can you tell me about Harriman that might point me in the right direction?"

Janice Bigelow knew next to nothing. Aside from her retelling of the affairs, she repeated the same story about the day of the kidnapping, and that was all. According to her, Don and Janice did very little talking during their liaisons. Janice claimed not to be much interested in Don's business affairs, and Don seemed primarily interested in Janice for her body. I walked away with no new leads; no new clues. Janice Bigelow left me with little more than complimentary teas and honey and a curiosity about who her diary informant was.

CHAPTER THIRTY-SEVEN

Suzanne wasn't home. I left her a phone message to call me as soon as she could. I wanted to get from her what she knew about Don's snooping around with those blueprints, and to find out anything else she might have come across. I also wanted to know that she was okay. Something big was brewing. While the facts were not yet evident, the noose was tightening around someone's neck. Murder meant they were hardballers. They would not go quietly. Renita and I were not fair game. Disposing of us would only draw more undesirable attention to something these people needed to remain concealed. I had an inkling why that was, and Harriman's murder wasn't the number one reason.

Renita was due to return from Seattle the next day. I had hoped to have talked with Suzanne by then. There was someone else I needed to see in the meantime. I called. He wasn't in. I left an urgent message on his voice messaging service to make certain I got his attention.

CHAPTER THIRTY-EIGHT

I was on my way to my lunch engagement when the car phone rang.

"C. J.?" said the voice from the other end. There was a jerky pause. "C. J., I need your help." The voice was hushed and frightened. "They're after me."

"Suzanne?" I said.

"Something terrible has happened, C. J." Her voice trailed off as if she had turned away from the phone. "It's all because of that *damn* diary."

"What about the diary? And who's after you? What's going on, Suzanne?"

"I'm at the Dunkin' Donuts on Sandy Boulevard. Can you meet me here?"

"I'll be there in fifteen minutes."

"Make it ten and I'll stick around. Otherwise, I'm on the move."

"Ten it is." The phone went dead. I stepped on the gas, canceling my lunch engagement as I maneuvered through traffic.

***

I rushed inside Dunkin' Donuts to find Suzanne tucked away at a table in the far corner nearest the back door. Suzanne was hunched down in her seat as if she were trying to make herself melt into the chair. When Suzanne saw me, she frantically motioned me to her like a woman desperately trying to fan cool her scalded tongue. I moved swiftly to her. There was a full cup of steaming black coffee in front of her and a picked-over bear claw. I sat across from her. Suzanne reached across the table, grabbed my hands with both of hers, and held on tight. She was trembling.

Suzanne was wearing a white wool blazer over a man's pinstriped dress shirt, along with dark blue jeans. Her black silky hair rose from the top of her head in a pronounced ponytail. Her cowrie shell bracelet, necklace, and earrings all looked handmade. She wore soft pink blush with matching lipstick, both of which stood out sharply against her color-drained face. Little pools of tear-diluted mascara were forming in the corners of her eyes. For an instant, we sat quietly staring at each other. This was her show. I waited for Suzanne to speak.

"It took you long enough," she tersely whispered. "I was about to leave."

"I got here as fast as I could. According to my watch, it's been less than ten minutes."

"Okay, whatever," Suzanne said with as much sarcasm as she could muster. She was scared, but her voice was angry. "Someone is after me."

"What makes you say that?"

"Because somebody broke into my apartment."

"How do you know it wasn't thieves?"

"The place was trashed and nothing was missing. They were looking for the diary, I'm telling you."

"How can you be so certain, Suzanne?"

"I just am, C. J." Her voice rose with frustration. The two teenagers behind the glass display counter glanced our way. Suzanne lowered her voice back to a whisper when she spoke. "Why else would someone destroy my apartment and not steal anything? Since I got involved with Don Harriman, my life's gone to shit."

"Why don't we get out of here? I'll take you back to your place and we can have a look around."

"Look around for *what?*"

"For clues on who might have ransacked your apartment."

Suzanne withdrew from me while tightening her grip even more.

"I'm not sure I want to go back there," she said with discernible apprehension.

"You're going to have to go home eventually; the sooner the better. I'll be with you all of the way. Did you call the police?"

"No, I just ran. I don't even remember if I closed my door."

"No problem, we'll call the police from my car." Her trembling had subsided. Fear seemed to be replaced with anxiety.

Suzanne looked around for a moment and took a deep swallow before she said, "Okay."

We stood together; in part because Suzanne wouldn't let go of my hands. I pried one hand loose to put an arm around her shoulders. Suzanne moved with tiny steps, as if I were escorting her to the gallows. In a calm voice, I assured her she had nothing to fear. I locked Suzanne safely in my car before getting in myself. Tension showed in her body and on her face. Her eyes kept darting about as if she were on the lookout for would-be assassins. After everything she'd been through of late, who could blame her?

CHAPTER THIRTY-NINE

We sat in my car in the Dunkin' Donuts parking lot for several minutes. I saw no need to take Suzanne back to some place that would—for the moment—only cause her more anxiety. She needed time to distance herself from the fear that kept forcing its way back into her psyche. I turned on the radio. Carmen McCrae sang "Straighten Up and Fly Right." It took close to an hour of jazz, smooth jazz, and light conversation before Suzanne regained her composure.

We made the short drive to Suzanne's apartment from the Dunkin' Donuts in eight minutes. Once we arrived in the parking lot of her apartment complex, we stayed in my car, talking. Suzanne had calmed enough that I felt it was safe to pursue an itching curiosity.

"There's something that doesn't add up here, Suzanne."

"Like what?" There was no tension in her voice. Suzanne sounded like a serious side of her old self.

"Why are you so sure it was someone after the diary who ransacked your place?"

"What else could it be?"

"Pissed off anybody lately?"

"Yes, but nobody that would do anything other than tell me where to go and how to get there."

"What about that ex-boyfriend you told me about? The one you recently dumped."

"*Him*," Suzanne snorted. "He's moved on. Last I heard, he was seeing some sophomore at PSU."

"Robber?"

"They didn't steal anything, remember?"

"Random vandalism is another possibility."

"Does that happen inside people's homes?"

"Occasionally."

"I doubt if that was the reason behind what they did to mine."

"Why would Alice Baker be so certain you have her dead husband's diary?"

"I never said it was Alice Baker."

"Who else could it be?"

"Maybe it was one of the women in the diary who sent some thugs to find it—or me."

"How would they know?"

Suzanne sat silent. A suspicion grew to a thought that burst into a realization. "Suzanne, you didn't!"

"Didn't what?"

"You didn't try to extort money from the women in that diary."

"I believe the word is 'blackmail'," Suzanne said, trying to play the whole thing off as if it were a joke.

"*Are you crazy?*"

"Maybe a little." Suzanne paused as she looked away from me, let out a long sigh, and turned back to me. "So I got a little greedy. I saw an opportunity to make some cheddar, and I took it."

"We're dealing with killers, here. If making yourself a target isn't enough, you've turned yourself into a criminal, as well?"

"You're not going to bust me, are you?"

"Why shouldn't I?"

Suzanne thought for a moment. "Let's make a deal. If I promise never to try anything like that again—or anything remotely like it—will you cut me a break?"

"This isn't skipping class or cheating on an exam. This is breaking the law in a big way. I have to mention this to the investigating officer."

Suzanne sat silent. Her face was taut with anger; her eyes electric with concern. There was no doubt I felt sorry for her. She did a stupid thing. Beyond the criminal ramifications, Suzanne had gambled with her life. I decided to help her, but not before letting her sweat a little.

"How'd you go about it?" I said, breaking the silence.

"You mean you want to hear about my extortion plan?" Her tone was grim and cautious.

"Only the highlights. Who did you contact?"

"Janice Bigelow and Charlotte Dolman."

"They were the only two?"

"Yes."

"Why just those two?"

"Because they were local, and I knew how to get in touch with them."

"What did you tell them?"

"Different things. I told Charlotte Dolman I wanted thirty thousand dollars in small unmarked bills or I was going to tell Alice Harriman—I mean Alice Baker—about her affair with her husband. I doubled the price on Janice Bigelow."

"Giving the working woman with a family a discount."

"You've got it," Suzanne said in a derisive voice.

"How thoughtful," I said, not sounding or feeling amused. "What made them believe you?"

"I don't follow."

"What proof did you have?"

"I quoted them a couple of juicy passages from the diary."

"You have the diary memorized?"

Her silence answered my question. "You copied the diary, didn't you?"

Suzanne nodded.

"*Damn it, Suzanne*, what the hell were you thinking?"

"I don't know. It seemed like easy money. I've been working my tail off for so long, trying to make ends meet while I follow my dream; and then this island of respite dropped into my lap. Why shouldn't I have a little cheddar so I could relax and stay focused on my art?"

"Because you have a conscience that would have eventually gotten the better of you."

"My conscience can't pay the bills. I would've dealt with it."

"Have you ever done anything like that before?"

"Of course not!"

"I didn't think so. If you had, you would know everything you do boomerangs back to you in one form or another. You never escape that fact."

"Is that the way it is with you?"

I immediately flashed back to my DEA days. My gut tightened. A haunting montage of tragic scenes from the underbelly of life raced through my memory. I leaned in close to Suzanne and spoke with firm conviction. "Every day of my adult life, that's the way it's been."

That statement unnerved Suzanne. I put us back on track in regards to her blackmail attempt. "Did they agree to pay?" I asked, removing the firmness from my voice while maintaining a serious tone.

"No," Suzanne said, after a swallow. "As a matter of fact, they laughed at me. They told me to go ahead and tell Alice Baker. She's bound to find out sooner or later anyway."

"They were right. Did you tell them who you were?"

"No, I'm not stupid."

"The jury's still out on that. Did you disguise your voice when you called?"

"I used that handkerchief over the mouthpiece trick, and made my voice sound deeper than normal. Plus, I used a payphone."

"You kept the calls short."

"Less than a minute. Since I'd met them while working at the Harriman's, I didn't want to take a chance of them getting a fix on me. Besides, that deep voice thing hurts."

"Either one or both of them found out who you were."

"What are we going to do about it?" Suzanne asked.

"*We?*"

"You're not going to leave me hanging, are you?"

"Give me one good reason why I shouldn't."

"Because you care about me, C. J.—not in the way I would like, but you do. I probably remind you of somebody close to you."

"I hadn't realized I was that obvious."

"All men are easy to read if you know how to look. It's only when women like what we see that we respond." *Another quote for the book of 'Why I'll Never Understand Women,'* I thought.

"First off, you're going to give me every copy you have of the diary."

"I only have one."

I looked at Suzanne. She stared back. "What?" she said.

"Just making certain you're telling the truth. Next, you're going to tell the investigating officer everything you told me about your blackmail scheme."

Alarmed, Suzanne said: "*Won't that incriminate me?*"

"Without question. It'll also be your best bet to be exonerated. I know this detective. As long as she believes you're being straight with her, she'll be straight with you. She won't use the blackmail information unless she needs to. If I don't miss my guess, she won't have to."

"What else?" Suzanne sounded like a pouting child still unwilling to accept her punishment.

"You're going to pack a bag and go home to your parents until it's time for you to go to New York."

"Why?" Suzanne whined.

"Because it's too dangerous here. If the person or persons who ransacked your place had found you here, we might not be having this conversation. Get my drift?"

"All too clearly." Suzanne looked scared again. *Good*, I thought. *She needed a wake-up call.*

"Don't worry, they won't come looking for you once you're out of town."

"How do you know?"

"I have a plan."

"If you have a plan that's going to keep those people off my back, then why do I have to leave town?"

"You know, you are a lot like my niece: quick-witted and stubborn. Only, she wouldn't be dumb enough to try to blackmail anyone."

"Are you sure?"

"Positive."

Suzanne scoffed.

"As a precaution against you winding up dead, you're leaving town. No further explanation required."

"You are not my father."

"What do you think your father will say when I call him to tell him what kind of danger you're in?"

"You don't have his number."

"You're kidding, right? I'm a private investigator. Getting your dad's number will be a piece of cake."

Suzanne looked pissed. "I'll go. But I'm not promising I won't come back."

"Promise me you won't come back until I give you the word that it's safe."

Suzanne scrunched up her face in thought. Just like my teenage niece, she was figuring her angles. "Deal," she said.

"Promise."

"I said 'deal'. It's the same thing."

"We both know that's not true. A deal is an informal agreement. A promise is a contract."

Suzanne made a sound that could only be described as exasperation. "I promise," Suzanne said, after a brief pause. We shook on it. While Suzanne showed signs of returning to her feisty self, I was considering who might have tossed her place.

CHAPTER FORTY

I telephoned Destini on my smartphone before we entered Suzanne's apartment, informing her about the ransacking and mentioning to her how that crime may have a possible connection to the Harriman case. Destini said she was on her way.

Suzanne's apartment was in shambles. Whoever tossed the place seemed more hell-bent on destruction than finding the diary. Much of her original artwork had been destroyed. Suzanne wept as we surveyed the damage. I felt sorry for her, but I couldn't help thinking that it could have been much worse. Her corpse could have been amongst the debris of her life.

Destini arrived shortly after we had entered Suzanne's apartment. I was still in the throes of comforting Suzanne. I did most of the talking, explaining not only what happened, but also what precipitated it. Destini took Suzanne off to the side to take down her statement while I had a look around.

Destini agreed to keep quiet about Suzanne's failed blackmail scheme unless circumstances merited otherwise. I also mentioned to the detective that there was no need to remain silent about the diary. We all agreed it might prove best to let the genie out of the bottle. That way, whoever was behind Don Harriman's murder and the ransacking of Suzanne Kwong's apartment would know that the evidence someone obviously feared coming to light was in the hands of prosecuting authorities. Once Destiny released news of the discovery of the diary, those who had killed for it would be forced into a 'wait and see' mode. At least, that's what we hoped. I would have lost my edge; but only for a moment. I had other cards to play.

"C. J., may I have a word with you in private?" Destini asked.

"Sure, excuse us, Suzanne," I said. Suzanne responded to Destini's reassuring smile with a nervous one as we stepped away out of earshot.

"After forensics gave the condo a thorough going over," Destini said, "I went back to have another look around."

"And?"

"The place had been ransacked." I involuntarily glanced at Suzanne. She was agonizing over the ruins, gingerly picking over pieces of shattered sculptures and shredded canvases.

"Someone desperately wants that diary, C. J."

"Maybe even bad enough to kill for it."

The three of us left together. Suzanne stuffed as many of her so-called necessities into one large suitcase and a tote as would fit. I drove Suzanne to the airport and put her on a plane for home. I assured her not to worry about her things or the apartment. Renita and I would take care of everything. She thanked me with a firm hug around the waist. When Suzanne looked up at me, she stared into my eyes like a lover longing for a kiss. So I kissed her right in the middle of her forehead. Suzanne gave me a smirk before letting go.

"Have a safe trip. And call me when you get there."

"All right, Uncle C. J.," Suzanne said with an attitude. I had to smile. So did Suzanne.

"They even destroyed that sketch I did of you in your office." Suzanne looked sad. "Ripped it to shreds."

"You can do another one when we see each other again."

"Promise?"

I paused as if giving it some thought.

"Deal," I said.

"That's not the same as a promise, and you know it."

I paused again, staring at her face. She patiently stared back. Suzanne had washed away the blush, and the light pink of her lips were their natural hue. Her color had returned. Her skin glowed with its resurrection; a glow that also emanated from her eyes. This young woman was going to make it big in this world. I could tell. Suzanne had been blessed with TBB: talent, brains and beauty. Her biggest obstacle would be herself. Those same qualities could be misdirected toward self-destruction just as easily as success.

"I promise," I said with sincerity.

Suzanne jumped up and kissed me on the cheek. She left with a smile and gait that told me Suzanne Kwong was going to be all right.

CHAPTER FORTY-ONE

Renita arrived at the office late the next day. She had phoned me from home at about eight the previous night to inform me she had just gotten back from Seattle. Renita gave me a brief overview of her interviews and told me she would fill me in on the particulars in the morning. Renita also mentioned she would arrive late to the office. Ernest wanted to treat her to a welcome home dinner at Fullman's. Renita made it clear that dinner might not be all that was on the menu for the night.

I had worked out in our office exercise room, showered, shaved, dressed, and was adding the Suzanne Kwong incident to the Harriman case file when Renita arrived an hour and a half late. Renita wore jeans, sneakers, and an old T-shirt, as I had suggested. The T-shirt was loose. The jeans were form-fitting. I wondered if Renita had any pants that didn't fit like a second skin.

We settled into the Harriman case after we dispensed with Renita's flirting, a general recap of her night with Ernest, and her supposed good time in Seattle.

The two married western Washington women were petrified about their adulterous affairs becoming public record, according to Renita; their spouses finding out being their number one concern. The single woman had an attitude similar to Suzanne's. She could care less if what she and Harriman did in private surfaced. It was all just wholesome adult fun, as far as she was concerned.

When I pressed Renita about whether she thought any of the married women could be moved to murder, based on their fear, Renita emphatically said no. Renita could not dredge up means or opportunity on any of the women; nor did she have a sense that any of them wanted Harriman dead.

"To be honest," Renita said, "I believe they all knew it wouldn't last. Add to that the fact that none of them was aware Harriman was having an affair with anyone else and you eliminate any jealousy motive or the theory of a woman scorned. The single woman was that way by choice. 'Not interested in a husband or kids; only my career' is how she put it. All of the women were in it for the sex.

"When Harriman walked into the lives of these married women, they were sexually frustrated. He made sex fun again. Their affair with Harriman translated back to their bedrooms and resurrected a sunken ship, so to speak. Why they kept seeing him afterwards? They honestly couldn't say."

I trusted my partner's judgment. We scratched Harriman's western Washington women from our list of possible murder suspects, barring no new evidence to the contrary.

I told Renita about Suzanne. Renita was pissed. She was ready to kick ass. I convinced Renita to settle for helping me clean Suzanne's apartment while we foraged for clues. Renita was glad to help.

I phoned Destini from my car phone on the way to Suzanne's apartment. I wanted to check to make certain it was all right for us to go inside. Destini said her people had come and gone and it was safe to go ahead with our plans. The only evidence the detectives had so far were that two men, about six-four and five-eight, weighing in at about 220 to 185 pounds respectively, appeared to have done all of the damage to Suzanne's apartment, according to the footprints Forensics had gathered from the carpet impressions. The men wore construction boots and gloves, so there were no fingerprints.

Destini had questioned a few of the neighbors. The people they questioned hadn't heard or seen anything. Destini, Renita and I were all thinking the same thing. The men who rifled Suzanne's apartment could be the same men who kidnapped—and possibly murdered—Don Harriman. Destini also made a wisecrack about when we were done with Kwong's place, hers could use a little sprucing up, as well. I told Destini I would be glad to clean house, but it was going to cost her. Destini playfully complained about me cleaning for a near stranger for free, but she had to negotiate in order to receive the same service.

"The difference is," I was quick to tease, "this is a one shot deal for Suzanne. For you, my offer stands for life."

Renita said, "Please." I ignored Renita.

"I'm going to have the chance to take you up on that offer one day, Mr. Cedric Joseph Cavanaugh." I knew Destini was referring to my still-AWOL marriage proposal. I didn't know what to say on the matter, so I pulled back to safer ground.

"Anything else we need to know about what happened at Suzanne's place?" I asked Destini.

"All right, C. J.," Destini said. "I'll let you off the hook this time. The answer is no. The lab people are in the process of doing their thing—you know the bit. We won't have any results for at least a couple of days. I'll let you know if anything comes up."

"Thanks." I paused for a moment. "You know I love you," I said. Renita rolled her eyes, folded her arms, and stared out of the passenger window.

"Of that, I have no doubt," Destini said. "And just for the record, I feel exactly the same way."

"You can't even say it, can you?" I said.

"Not at work," Destini said. "Gotta' go. Bye!"

Destini hung up. I had to chuckle.

"So what's the deal?" Renita asked, not wanting to prolong the agony of what she had just overheard.

"We clean, Renita. We clean."

CHAPTER FORTY-TWO

Suzanne's apartment looked worse than when I last saw it. The old tornado analogy my mother used when describing my room when I was a teenager came to mind. Renita and I had decided to place all of her art in a storage unit we rented nearby on her behalf. While most of her life's work had been destroyed, a few pieces had survived. We felt it best to allow Suzanne the choice of what was worth keeping or salvaging and discarding, no matter how painful the call. If she needed us during that time, we would be there for her.

We spent the morning transporting her art to the storage facility, broke for lunch, then spent most of the afternoon making Suzanne's place spotless. Our quest for additional clues was fruitless. We used what remained of the afternoon to canvas the neighborhood, coming up with only bits and pieces that didn't amount to much.

Renita had tried giving me the impression she was partying in Seattle to mess with my head, but I knew differently. To gather the amount of information Renita had on those western Washington women in the short amount of time I'd given her, Renita had to be hustling.

"Thanks for the lift, C. J.," Renita said as I pulled into her driveway. "Care to come in for a cup of coffee or a glass of wine?" Renita was in all-out flirt mode. Her eyes were simmering with wicked mischief. Why? Who knows?

"No, thank you."

"Are you sure?" Renita reached up as if to slip her hand behind my neck. I intercepted her attempt by grabbing her wrist and easing her hand into her lap. She smiled drowsily.

"Cat-like reflexes. I like that in a man." The last few days had been hectic for her, and I knew firsthand how that could wear on a person.

"You can take tomorrow off, if you want. I can manage one day without you."

"Really? It would give me a chance to catch up on my beauty sleep. Thanks, C. J. I'll give you a call in the morning to let you know whether I'm coming in or not."

Just before she got out of the car, I made the mistake of asking Renita a loaded question. "Was it the trip or Ernest that wore you out?"

Renita gave me a naughty smile and said, "Both."

I drove back toward the office, considering my next move. There were suspicions I needed to confirm. The only question was where to begin. I decided to keep Alice Baker company for a while.

CHAPTER FORTY-THREE

The day was clear and sunny. The temperature hovered in the mid-eighties with very little humidity. It was a beautiful summer day in Portland. The type of day that made one forget about the incessant rain and overcast skies. It was the type of day that made the Northwest sparkle. Everywhere were blossoms making their presence known. A complete array of fertile, colorful beauty was on full display. Even in the hectic midst of downtown Portland during rush hour, flowers, trees, and sunlight helped create equanimity amongst the dogged fray. It was a day tailor-made for me to be at play with my terriers in the park.

I staked out Alice Baker instead. Or rather, I staked out her car at her office in hopes that Ms. Baker might lead me to additional clues.

I was playing a hunch—or maybe it was more like an inkling. Aside from my investigator's intuition on the true motive behind Harriman's murder, I had nothing in the way of proof. I needed hard evidence; indisputable facts to validate my unsubstantiated suspicions. The question was, would Alice Baker ever provide me with any.

At 6:17 p.m., I followed Alice Baker to a Blue Sun office building construction site in southeast Portland. Alice Baker met with the site foreman, Lenny Downs. I had to observe their meeting from my car. If I tried getting any closer, not only would I run the risk of Alice Baker recognizing me, but the foreman might, as well. He was one of the people I had interviewed while playing photographer/reporter. The foreman's alibi had checked out. He had been working during the time of the kidnapping, as well as the murder. His assistant, Brian Kephart, substantiated that fact. Kephart claimed to have never left the foreman's side during the times I had mentioned.

The meeting lasted twenty minutes. The foreman appeared to give Alice Baker an on-site progress report. Ms. Baker seemed pleased with what she heard.

By 6:53, Ms. Baker was home. She stayed there for forty-four minutes. She emerged wearing blue jeans, sneakers, a gray short-sleeved sweatshirt, a Seattle Mariners baseball cap, dark sunglasses, and a Gucci shoulder bag.

Alice Baker led me to the Wayfarer's Inn, a bargain motel on the outskirts of Beaverton. She parked and then made a beeline to a room on the top level at the southwest corner. Alice knocked twice, waited about five seconds, then knocked three times. The door opened. Alice Baker hurried inside. Someone I couldn't see had let her in.

I considered going up to the room to see what I could see, and to listen outside the door, but decided against it. Even with the encroaching darkness, it was too risky. I parked my car where I could see the entrance to the room Alice Baker had entered. The blinds were closed. Even with the lights on, I couldn't make out who was inside. I made myself comfortable and waited.

Alice Baker stayed for a little more than two hours. I stuck around after she had left. I wanted to see who Alice had met. Ten minutes later, two men sauntered out, both dressed in dusty construction gear. I recognized them immediately: Alan Slankard and Larry "Tadpole" Paulozzo. Slankard said something over his shoulder to someone still inside the room. I waited. Thirteen minutes later, Janice Bigelow emerged, followed six minutes later by John Ullock. Aside from the killers (and probable kidnappers), the gang was all there.

I waited another few minutes. Night had fallen, but the outdoors lighting did its job. I had to be certain there were no other revelations held up in that motel room. I went up to the room and knocked two times, waited five seconds, and then knocked three times. No one answered. I pressed my ear to the door and listened for a minute. Not a sound. The door was unlocked, but that wouldn't have stopped me. I let myself in. The place was empty. Besides a few empty food containers, water and beer bottles, there was nothing to see. I slipped out. I had one more stop to make before I left.

The motel desk clerk was a college student who chewed her gum like she was gnawing it into submission. Her geology homework was laid out on a small metal desk a few short paces directly behind the check-in counter. I assumed she was working part-time to make ends meet. I asked about the room. She tried playing it by the book. I applied a little incentive in the form of one hundred dollars. She turned away as I checked the register.

The room was leased to Blue Sun Real Estate. They kept it on retainer for out-of-town guests, the clerk mentioned. *Judging by the out-of-the-way location of the motel, that room could only serve as a hideaway for clandestine guests, or for stealth meetings like the one I just witnessed*, I thought. I thanked the desk clerk with another hundred and a vow of silence about where I got the information— a promise I fully intended to keep.

'Interesting' would not have begun to describe what I thought at that moment. I had figured Al and Tadpole were somehow involved with the Harriman mess, but Janice Bigelow and John Ullock were a riddle.

It was late and I was tired. I decided to go home, have a late meal and hot shower, and get a good night's sleep. Alice Baker had provided me with enough surprises for one day. Tomorrow would be soon enough to try to fit those two new pieces into the puzzle.

CHAPTER FORTY-FOUR

Early morning brought with it a few aimless white clouds that posed no threat of rain. The temperature was on the shallow side of seventy, but steadily rising. The humidity was negligible. Booker and Andrew and I had a great morning run. After my shower, the twins and I ate breakfast. I fed my tropical fish and Zebra finches, then meditated for close to an hour. I played back what I knew regarding the Harriman murder case as I dressed for work. I then added to that information what I suspected. The summary results netted more questions than answers.

When I entered the office, to my surprise, Renita was already hard at work. I had obviously underestimated her resiliency. Renita was documenting her report on the women she had interviewed in western Washington. I poked my head into her office. Renita said good morning while she continued tapping away at her computer keys. I went to my office to write my report on what I had witnessed the day before.

Renita had a good deal more information to convey in her reports than I did in mine. I finished before her. I had wanted to meet with Renita to go over what we had, and also, to decide in which direction we were going to move in. I waited. While I did, I contacted the lunch date that I'd previously cancelled due to Suzanne Kwong's emergency. I was contemplating whether to wait until the end of business that day to inform Destini what I had witnessed at the motel when in walked Renita, ready to talk, with her investigator notepad in hand.

She sat in the visitor's chair opposite my desk, crossed her legs, opened her notepad, and extracted the silver pen from its pen loop.

"No recordings?" I asked.

"They wouldn't let me."

I nodded. "People have a propensity to be more forthcoming when you're taking notes, anyway. Recordings have a tendency to make some people nervous, more closed off, and even a bit paranoid. With notes, the interviewee unwittingly harbors a belief of deniability if the interview becomes untenable. It gives them a false sense of control over the situation. That's tougher to do with a recording."

Renita shrugged her shoulders. "I guess."

"What about hard copies of your reports? You did write them, didn't you?"

"Of course, but I prefer to read from my handwritten notes, if you don't mind."

I understood even if Renita didn't. There's something tangible about reviewing your handwritten notes that transports you right back to the interview. For whatever reason, that connection erodes during the translation from notepad to official report, somehow sterilizing the experience. I suppose, in the end, that's precisely the result you want.

"Here are the highlights," Renita said. "Shirley Faber, married, no children, self-employed as a real estate agent, lovely, fit, and personable. She works primarily to relieve the boredom of being a bank president's trophy wife, and her real estate commissions provide her with a little mad money. She met Harriman at a real estate conference in Seattle. He was handsome, charming, and available, according to Mrs. Faber. Her husband was in New York on business that week. They wound up in Harriman's hotel room. The sex was good, so she kept going back for more. She and Harriman managed to steal away three to four times a month. Harriman had a little getaway on Bainbridge Island where they would meet. According to Mrs. Faber, their affair was still ongoing right up until his death. Around the time Harriman was kidnapped and eventually murdered, her and her husband were in France on a second honeymoon.

"And before you ask, I did pay a visit to his Bainbridge hideaway. The caretaker hadn't heard from or seen Don Harriman for a few days prior to his murder."

"Conclusions?"

"In my opinion, Shirley Faber didn't do it. If her alibi checks out, the time frame doesn't match."

"She could have hired the men who did the crime?"

"She lacks the independent resources—and doubtful connections—to employ those kinds of professionals. Although, I will say this: the news of Harriman's death seemed to affect her about as much as a broken fingernail."

I nodded. Renita continued. "Two things all of these women had in common when it came to Harriman: they didn't love him, and they did not know he kept a diary. When I told Mrs. Faber about the diary, she turned white as a ghost. Her biggest distress was her husband finding out about the diary, divorcing her, and leaving her penniless."

"Are you suggesting she's a gold digger?"

"That's affirmative."

"Wasn't she concerned Harriman might let something slip?"

"Nope. According to Mrs. Faber, he had a lot more to lose than she did."

"She obviously didn't know about his personal fortune."

"Or the fact that Harriman actually loved his wife."

The recaps of the Melanie Collins and Jennifer Norton interviews were the same in form, but varied in content. Mrs. Collins was a striking account executive for a large advertising agency. She was married, with two children. The news of Harriman's death had saddened her, but not to the point of distraction. She credited their affair for salvaging her sex life and thereby saving her ten-year marriage. Her only concern regarding Harriman's diary was it being grounds for divorce by the man she loved.

Jennifer Norton was a single, beautiful, multi-millionaire blogger, app writer, and software engineer who described herself as fiercely independent and a self-proclaimed hedonist. Ms. Norton cared less about the existence of a diary or it being made public.

"She even asked for a copy," Renita said. "She thought it might make for interesting blogging content. And I believed her. Ms. Norton did say she would miss Don, because of the great sex."

In Renita's opinion, her biggest concern was filling Harriman's bedroom spot on her pleasure card.

Melanie Collins and Jennifer Norton clearly did not have either sufficient motives, opportunities, or connections to have Harriman kidnapped or killed, according to Renita. None of the western Washington women panned out as viable suspects in our murder investigation.

Renita silently made a final pass through her notes, looking for anything she may have forgotten to mention. "Any thoughts?" she asked when she was done.

"What about the husbands?"

"As far as I could tell, they're completely in the dark."

"So there's no chance they could have known about the affairs?"

"No way that I can see. Do you think I should interview them?"

I gave the idea a moment's thought. "That won't be necessary. Sounds to me like you covered everything. I may have something once I've read your official reports. Good job."

"I know, C. J. I'm not just another pretty face with a hot bod. I want to give my reports one last review before printing you a copy. I know how you prefer to read these things on paper," Renita said, wearing an impish smile.

"Is that a dinosaur dig?"

"I'm not suggesting any such thing, but the paperless office has arrived—it's time to catch up."

"So that's why you used a *notepad* instead of an *iPad* on those interviews."

"A bad habit I've obviously picked up from you."

"Not the first, and probably not the last."

"That's for sure. If you keep this up, I may need therapy."

"Until such time, I look forward to reading your final reports *on paper,* if you don't mind. We do still stock that antiquated material, don't we?"

"And red pens, too."

There were no loopholes in what Renita told me regarding those western Washington women. I would hold off officially eliminating them from our suspect pool until I read Renita's final reports. We couldn't do anything to help those who were concerned about disclosure of the Harriman diary. All bets were off once we turned it over to the police. All we could do was ask the DA for discretion once the case went to trial on behalf of those innocent women, if the need arose to release that vaunted memoir. Destini could be counted on to do her best to keep all inquiries private. She would also do whatever was necessary to get the job done.

"Either Janice Bigelow or Charlotte Dolman fingered Suzanne Kwong to the people who were behind Harriman's murder," I said at the start of new business on the Harriman case. "It's clear to me that whoever rifled Suzanne's apartment had expected to find a lot more than the recounting of sex stories in Harriman's diary."

I also told Renita about the meeting at the Wayfarer's Inn. I had no answers for Renita when pressed for my thoughts regarding the motel meeting. My groundless speculations weren't worth mentioning. Renita said she didn't like where our case was heading. I agreed. There was an odor to it, like the suffocating stench of a slaughterhouse. We had stumbled onto something: a murder that was bigger than its victim. Don Harriman hadn't been killed out of a jealous rage or violent fury. His death was a cold, calculated, business-like venture.

And there was the rub.

CHAPTER FORTY-FIVE

"If you wanted to work on your office computer from home, how would you go about it?" I asked Renita. Brilliant sunlight flooded my office. I was seated behind my desk. Renita sat across from me.

"VPN and Internet are the most common methods," Renita said. "We use VPN."

"How would you safeguard against intruders?" I asked. "How do you do it?"

"Passwords, firewalls, antivirus software—where are you going with this, C. J.?"

"According to the PPB lab, Harriman used a utility program to wipe his laptop clean of all information he didn't want recovered. He used scrubbing software similar to that used by the CIA and the Department of Defense."

"Disk scrubber software is fairly common these days. You can buy copies online. I scrub our computers and laptops before we donate or recycle them."

"Even an extra-strength scrubber that somehow renders the hard drive utterly useless, like the one Harriman used?"

"Sure, or something close. The best place to find nuke software is on the dark web."

"You mean besides the federal government?"

"Yes."

"Why would a real estate agent be so concerned about scouring his laptop?"

"Maybe he had some shady dealings he didn't want uncovered. Or maybe the people after him were somehow incriminated in his electronic files."

"Why would a man in the throes of danger waste precious time attempting to eradicate incriminating real estate files? It's not like he didn't have enough legal firepower to broker some sort of deal. What's the worst that would have happened? He'd lose his license. Be sent to a white-collar prison for a few years? Holding onto those allegedly implicating files would have been his bargaining chip. Those files—if they existed—could have saved his life."

"Maybe he was a blackmailer?"

"I thought of that. There's no evidence to support that theory. There was no inexplicable money trail. No illegal favors by anyone connected with Harriman."

"Maybe one of the women was blackmailing him."

"Again, no money trail."

"What about his lurid sex life? He could have coerced some of the women into having sex with him."

"You don't really believe that."

"No, but it's worth noting."

"His sex life might be deemed excessive, yes; but lurid, no. All of the women he made it with, that we've connected with, were willing participants."

"Obviously the man wasn't thinking clearly. It can get tense when someone's out to kill you. I know about that first hand. And so do you."

I thought about what Renita said. "The Gem Connection" case came to mind again. Both of our lives had been in peril. I nodded to Renita to let her know we were on the same wavelength. Renita gravely nodded in the affirmative.

There was a disquieting pause. Each of us privately reflected on a traumatic time in our shared professional past. We'd survived. We did better than survival. We came away victorious. Renita graduated to a full-fledged investigator during that time. I realized that I could still cut it in the dark heart of the manmade jungle.

Back to the case at hand: those killers were after something more than damning evidence of shady real estate dealings. Harriman had hooked a shark; a great white, in my opinion—one that had yanked him overboard before he could reel it in.

"It doesn't feel right," I said. "I believe Harriman was trained to react as he did with that laptop."

"What makes you say that?"

"In times of stress, we have a tendency to resort to that which we know best. Whatever our reflexes or training tells us to do, we gravitate toward.

'Automatic pilot', some people call it. Harriman believed he had only a few minutes to live. He must have heard the killers enter the house. He stopped what he was doing on his laptop and then initiated the scrubber software. Not knowing whether he had enough time for the program to complete its task, he tossed the laptop out of the window, expecting that whatever the program didn't abolish, the damage would be enough to finish the job."

"What was on his laptop that was worth dying for?"

"That's what we're still trying to determine. Maybe the answers are on that PC we found in his condo."

Our agendas for the day appeared to be simple. Renita was to finalize her western Washington report. When that was done, she was to go back to breaking down the information on Don Harriman's condo PC. My tasks were more field-oriented.

"I'll wring out every bit of data on that computer that I can," Renita said.

"Beauty and brains. Ernest is a lucky man."

"You'd be even more fortunate if you dumped Destini and gave me a chance."

"You're better off applying your energies toward Ernest." Renita twisted her mouth to one side. I ignored her irksome gesture. "So what do you say we get to work?"

"The PC data has been slow going up to now," Renita said, bouncing up out of her seat. "It may take a little while."

"No problem; that will give me time to do some leg work." I stood to leave.

"There's nothing wrong with your legs, from where I'm standing." Renita blocked my path. She looked me up and down in a salacious manner that women are much better at executing with class than men. There is no male defense mechanism for such a tactic. I took Renita firmly, but gently, by the arm and escorted her out of my office. Her only resistance was a playful smile. Renita retired to her office, taking her intimate fantasies with her. I had business to attend to. I left without saying another word.

CHAPTER FORTY-SIX

The Harriman case remained mine for the time being. Destini had been force fed another four homicides in the last two days and was only too grateful for the help. That meant we didn't have to hustle. The longer the killers remained free, the less likelihood they would be apprehended. I wasn't about to let them get away with murder, cold trail or not.

The lunch date I had rescheduled due to Suzanne Kwong's emergency stared across his broad office desk at me. Sunlight worked its way in through every crack and crevice of the partially opened vertical blinds. The walls of his office were covered with plaques, citations, awards, diplomas, and framed pictures of family, friends and colleagues. My picture was amongst them.

Patrick O'Malley was as tough as they come: a Harvard Law School grad with a blue-collar background. He was a freckled man with short hair brushed back in waves of carrot red and encroaching steel gray. His build was well muscled, except for a slight middle-aged paunch. (A genetic curse from his father, he claimed. I suspected his affection for dark Scottish Ale was more to blame.) Patrick had a calm, pleasant demeanor that made one feel at ease. An off-the-rack dark blue two-piece designer suit fit him nicely. The suit went well with his Mickey Mouse tie (a Father's Day gift from his youngest daughter, he confessed).

Patrick had what my dad would call chops, but they were actually muttonchops. His side whiskers came out narrow at the temples and broadened along his cheeks like red quarter notes. O'Malley hadn't always looked so musical. He didn't have chops when we first met more than twenty years ago.

I was a new stud on the DEA campus. Patrick was three years my senior. We didn't get along. I was stubborn, cocky, and at times, belligerent. Patrick was the same. We were partnered. I had my own ideas about how things should be done, as did Patrick: my way being more maverick; his way being strictly by the book. We got into a number of public disputes along the way, ranging from where to park the car to how to bring down a perp—disputes we led others to believe were minor disagreements in strategies.

The fistfights were what we kept private. Who won most of them? That depends on whom you ask. To outsiders, we were a dysfunctional team. To us, we were just hardheaded brothers who at times had a volatile way of settling our differences.

After five years as partners, we were reassigned to different regional offices. Patrick and I stayed in touch for a while. Then, as life would have it, we drifted apart. I ran into Patrick at D.C. headquarters on a fluke. It was a few years before my retirement. Patrick was there to accept an Assistant Director position in Tucson. I was there being primed for an undercover operation in South America. Patrick had a 2-inch scar across his right cheek, a little memento from a skirmish with a knife-wielding drug dealer he'd busted six months prior to our chance meeting. According to Patrick, it took the dealer three months to recover from the beating he gave him. My theory was that Patrick wore chops to hide his scar. He denied it. Patrick said it reminded him of his Irish roots and made him look damn handsome in the process.

I had worked with the Portland DEA Deputy Director as a consultant on several cases. We had reached the age where physical battles were reduced to friendly verbal jousts. His deep-set dark green eyes stayed on mine. His expression remained stoic as I explained to him how I became involved in the Harriman case. Patrick didn't react when I told him about finding his business card hidden away in the deceased's secret condo. Instead, he casually slid a No. 2 pencil between his right thumb and index finger, end over end, atop the felt green ink blotter on his desk.

Patrick sat quietly for a minute when I finished. He had averted his stare away from me. I knew him well enough to know that meant he was adding up what I had told him juxtaposed against what he already knew about the Harriman case. His lack of reaction told me two things: Patrick already knew about my involvement in the Harriman case, and his DEA training and years of experience couldn't hide the fact that he was surprised I'd found the connection between him and Don Harriman. The pencil gave him away. What I had learned about Patrick over the years—and never told him—was that when something startled or surprised him, he would settle himself by finding a prop to focus on. The pencil was his calming point.

"Harriman was working for us," Patrick said in his usual, even, measured tone. "In a manner of speaking, that is. Before I get to the present, let's clear up the past. Don Harriman was an ex-FBI agent. He was one of their best, except for one nagging problem."

"Let me guess. Women."

Patrick nodded. "He couldn't keep it in his pants. Harriman couldn't even draw the line between the women involved in his investigations and his libido. He was the key witness in a multiple murder case with strong connections to the mob. His testimony was thrown out when it was learned he was sleeping with the defendant's wife. That was the last straw for the Bureau."

I nodded. I didn't know what Patrick knew about Harriman's diary, but I guessed he had the whole story. It would not have surprised me if his people didn't have their own copy of the diary. What I knew was that Patrick never asked, and it wasn't my place to volunteer the information.

"About a month before Don Harriman was killed, he came to me saying he could get his hands on information that would be invaluable to the DEA."

"Illegal narcotics?"

"He didn't say, but that was my guess. Why else would anyone contact the DEA? Harriman asked if I were interested. I told him of course, and asked him to be more specific. Harriman told me to keep my pants on. I would know in time. All he would spill for certain was that it was big."

"What did he want in return?"

Patrick smiled. "You haven't forgotten the rules of engagement, I see."

"Guess not."

"He wanted me to broker a deal for him with the FBI to sanitize his record. He wanted his record to read that he resigned voluntarily after having served honorably."

"Did you do as he asked?"

"I told him—like I'm telling you—that I have no authority over FBI matters."

"I'm sure he bought that," I said sarcastically.

"He told me—and I quote — 'Bullshit! DEA and the FBI are always exchanging favors. I know. I used to be part of the mix. Now, do we have a deal or don't we?' I told him it depended on the information. If it was worth the phone call, then maybe. Harriman smiled a sly, satisfying smile like a salesman who had just sold something that would net him a big fat commission. We shook on it. He left. And that was the last I saw of him."

"You did speak to him."

"Twice a week, he'd call to let me know it was tougher than expected, but things were moving along."

"No specifics."

"None."

"Did you ever meet with Harriman in your office?"

"Once, when Harriman brought me his proposal."

I took a moment to ponder something. Patrick must have read my mind.

"Wondering why Harriman sent you that text message?" Patrick said.

"How'd you know about that?"

"Word gets around. I keep my ears open. Hear things."

"Any insight on what the text message Harriman sent me means?"

"I would have thought you'd have it figured out by now."

"I'll take that as a no."

Patrick nonchalantly shrugged. "You'd be right in that assertion."

"Okay, Patrick, what did you find out?"

"Pardon?"

"You didn't just sit around waiting for a phone call from Harriman. You put some of your people on him."

"I did no such thing," Patrick said in a way that would have convinced someone who didn't know him as well as I did that he was being sincere. "A stranger comes into my office spouting off about having valuable information—of which he proffered no details—and all he wanted in exchange was to have his FBI service record expunged. Aside from a lot of talk, Harriman never produced one shred of evidence of any illegal activities. How would I justify that expense to my district manager?"

"What do you think?

"About what?"

"Was Harriman onto something?"

"Definitely. What, I couldn't tell you."

"Could not, or will not?"

"You choose."

Patrick had managed to keep his poker face. His eyes didn't give him away, either. The only indicator I had that Patrick was holding back was the fact he kept playing with that damn pencil.

"I can't force you to tell me anything, Patrick. But as a friend, I'm asking you to give me something to chew on."

"I recommend you try that little shop on Alder near Rich's Cigars. They have excellent bagels."

Patrick and I both smiled. This wasn't personal. We both knew how the game was played. We were professionals. If he could tell me more, he would. That didn't mean I would stop trying to squeeze it out of him.

"Cleaning up his FBI record meant that much to Harriman?" I asked. Our smiles were gone. We had returned to our game faces.

"Apparently so."

"Did he give you any reasons?"

Patrick shook his head. There was a moment of contemplative silence. Patrick and I stared at each other, two warhorses sizing each other up.

"Is there more?" I asked.

"Such as?"

"Harriman's background was too clean. I never bought it. Everyone has blips on their radar. Some are hidden better than others. Harriman's past read like a Cliff Note version of a life—the type of clean that is more doctored than fact. It's the type of summary résumé you would find in grade school history books, or a simplified background a government agency would supply for one of their field operatives."

Patrick smiled. "You haven't lost your touch. Why don't you return to us, C. J.? We could use a good man like you back in the fold."

"I appreciate the offer, Patrick, but I've done my time with the DEA. I've seen enough of the worst of humankind. Going back to that life would be like committing suicide for me. That's something I'm just not going to do."

Patrick said he understood, but he left the door open in case I changed my mind.

"We scripted Harriman's past," Patrick said. "Nothing elaborate; the overview of most of what you learned as fact. We just plucked a fair amount of detailed information out. We needed to cover his ass in case any of the people he was snooping on got suspicious. You know how it works."

"All too well."

"And yes, Don Harriman was his real name," Patrick added before I could ask.

"So you think Harriman was really onto something?"

"Don't you?"

"Did he give you any names?"

Patrick shook his head.

"What about what he was looking for; any clue there?"

"Nothing. He kept saying that once he wrapped things up, we'd be the first to know."

"Did Harriman have a handler?" A DEA handler was a person who watched over field informants.

"No."

"Harriman reported directly to you?"

"Me, and only me. He wouldn't have it any other way."

"*Come on, Patrick*," I said. "Do you really expect me to believe you were in the dark on this?"

Patrick raised his hands as if surprised by my statement. It was an act, but a good one. If I didn't know him better, I would have bought it.

"You're telling me that an ex-FBI Investigator comes to you with a hunch about something involving illegal narcotics and you weren't all over it? I don't buy that for a second."

Patrick toyed with his pencil. His eyes stayed pinned to mine. His smile was slow in coming. "I'm afraid I've told you all I know on this one, C. J. We tried getting involved in what Harriman was doing, but he wouldn't let us in. He spotted us at every turn. Harriman told me to back off, or he'd drop his investigation and we'd never find out what was going on."

"And you believed him."

"Oh yeah. Harriman may have been a womanizer, but he was tough and smart. He wanted his FBI record cleared. Why, I've no idea. But whatever he was working on—at least, so he believed—was worth the trade-off."

"Any between-the-line reading on Harriman's diary?" I said.

"Diary? What diary?"

"And I suppose you don't know anything about the demolished laptop, or the computer we found in Harriman's hideaway condo, either?"

"Harriman had a hideaway condo? I'm not surprised, considering his out-of-control sex drive. I don't know anything about a laptop or a computer."

"Yes you do, Patrick. You know all about them. But I'll bet Harriman got one by you. At first, I thought the condo was just his playpen; which is what your people, who were keeping surveillance on him, thought. It's what I would have surmised had I been in their shoes. Harriman used his reputation to his advantage. He used his womanizing to mask his base of operation. I'm sure he paraded enough women into that condo to keep his reputation alive. Harriman also knew you wouldn't bother searching the condo because you would dismiss it as his love shack. Why bother? All you'd find in there was a missing earring or a lost pair of panties, right?"

Patrick continued to stare, not changing his expression or his mood.

"I'll bet it got to the point where you didn't watch the condo anymore."

"Let's just say for the sake of argument that what you say is true, C. J.— in regards to us being suckered by Harriman. What would we have found in his diary, or on his laptop, or on his condo PC?"

"You already know the answers, Patrick. The laptop was toast. The police lab confirmed that. The diary is just what it appears to be: a lascivious diversion to throw everyone off track. The computer information—" I stood to leave, "that, Patrick, was what I was hoping you could tell me about."

Patrick stood. We shook hands across his desk; the firm handshake of two confident men who respected one another.

"If I had anything that would help you in your investigation, C. J., I would have told you." Patrick was being honest to a point. He'd told me what he could. What he couldn't tell me was anything that would hamper ongoing DEA investigations or endanger the lives of any of his people. With that understanding, I dropped the matter.

"If I come across anything I think you can use," I said, "I'll make certain to pass it your way."

"I'd appreciate it. Let's not be strangers. It's been months since I've seen you. We're supposed to be friends. Friends don't neglect each other that long without so much as a hello. What say we get together for lunch next week to keep the fellowship ball rolling?"

That was Patrick's way of keeping tabs on me. He knew me well enough to know I would be straight with him on anything I turned up. Our lunch date was his way of making certain he kept himself in the loop without expending manpower to have me shadowed. Besides, I'd notice anyone he put on my tail and I'd be none too pleased about it.

"Sounds good," I said, "as long as you promise to stay away from any talk about me rejoining the DEA."

"Deal," Patrick said. We shook hands again.

"I'll give you a call to set up a lunch date."

"Just one more thing, C. J.," Patrick said, just before I opened his office door.

"I'll tell Renita you said hello," I said, beating Patrick to the punch. Patrick smiled like he did on those rare occasions he beat me at chess. I smiled back at him before I left.

CHAPTER FORTY-SEVEN

I stopped by the homes of Janice Bigelow, John Ullock, and Alice Baker. There were no answers. I was certain John Ullock was home. He had tried to sneak to the front door. Fortunately, for me, he moved like an elephant. I caught a quick glimpse of his eye through the peephole. He wasn't alone. Someone had asked him who it was. He whispered for them to keep quiet. Both remained stock-still in the hall, as if scared stiff by the bogie man. I couldn't see inside. I left. Whatever they were up to could await the bright light of full disclosure.

I circled the block and found a spot to park where I could observe the three houses without being observed. Lock pulled out of his garage about half an hour later. In the car with him was Janice Bigelow. They both appeared agitated. I wondered if it was caused by my unannounced visit or due to some residue from the clandestine gathering at the motel the other day.

They hurried off in the opposite direction of where I was parked. It was a powerful temptation. To follow, or not to follow—that was the question. I watched them disappear from sight, still pondering my choices. The temptation died. I elected to stick to my original plan. To make certain the odd couple weren't just making a quick junket, I waited a few minutes before I made my move.

I maneuvered my way to the rear of Alice Baker's house. At the back of her home, a large backyard patio was met by a bright green lawn that flowed into a curved berth of colorful flowers. Paneled behind the flower beds were roses, junipers, and myrtles. Walled just beyond the bushes and shrubs were evergreen and poplar trees. The trees were also the beginning of a bosk that blocked the back of the house from view. I looked around the yard and patio for signs of any clues. There was none that I could see.

Angled at approximately seventy degrees to the left and right of the patio were two concrete paths. They led into canopies of trestles covered by thick vines that made for natural tunnels. At the mouth of the tunnels the concrete paths stopped. Packed dirt floors took it from there.

I ventured along the path leading east. A skid mark cut deep into the concrete path where the notorious laptop had met its fate. I couldn't see through the vines once I entered the tunnel. It was almost as if I had stepped into a cave. Even the sharp sunlight could not pierce the dense black shade. I turned on the flashlight I had taken out of my car trunk and combed the area for clues. When I emerged at the other end, I stood approximately twenty paces from Lock's back patio. I retraced my steps.

Once back at Alice Baker's home, I ventured along the path leading in the opposite direction. This time I emerged about twenty paces from the patio of Janice Bigelow. Of course, it had been so easy. Why hadn't I thought of it before?

CHAPTER FORTY-EIGHT

My meeting with Patrick had answered a number of questions. For one, I now knew how Harriman got a bead on me. My photograph was amongst those on Patrick's walls. Harriman must have seen it and recognized me. With his FBI background, it would have been elementary for him to find out what he wanted to know about me without arousing suspicion. What Harriman discovered made him believe he could trust me as a safety valve in case whatever he was investigating blew up in his face.

Harriman had obviously underestimated how quickly things could go down. He clearly thought he would have more breathing room. If he had a plan to forward his information to me, he did not have time to implement it. Harriman improvised. The text message was the best he could do.

Renita was hard at work on the Harriman PC data when I poked my head into her office.

"I know how they kidnapped Harriman," I said, and then went to my office. Renita darted into my office as I made myself comfortable. She sat across from me. Renita was as eager to hear what I had to say as a child on Christmas Eve.

"I'm all ears."

"Suzanne Kwong said that when she saw the kidnappers, it looked as though they were about to kill Harriman. That was the plan. Whether the intruders got the information out of Harriman or not, they wanted him dead. Only, they wanted to murder Harriman in his home. They probably intended to make it look like a burglary gone wrong. Suzanne spoiled their plans—and prolonged Harriman's life.

"Bigelow and Ullock went inside to help buy time for the kidnappers to take Harriman to one of their homes by way of the covered paths in their backyards. They kept Harriman there until the coast was clear. Then the kidnappers took Harriman somewhere else. They tortured him, making one last stab at forcing him to tell them what he knew. Harriman wouldn't comply, so they killed him. And that's not all."

I filled Renita in on my meeting with Patrick. Renita took it all in with quiet amazement.

"Harriman was full of surprises," Renita said when I was done.

"The fact that his murderers are still hot to find out what Harriman knew means it's still out there. It's up to us to find it first. Any headway on those files?"

Renita shifted in her chair. "Being former FBI explains how Harriman got his hands on high-end customized software."

"I don't follow."

"I was having a tough time breaking Harriman's encrypted files, so I contacted a friend of mine at the NSA," Renita said. "His specialty is breaking computer encryptions. I sent along a couple of Harriman's files to let him have a go at them. It turned out Harriman was using an old NSA computer file scrambler. My friend placed a copy of the software on my website, I downloaded it, ran it, and *bam*. We're in like Snoop Dogg at a players' convention."

"This friend of yours gave you a copy of NSA software?"

"Don't worry, C. J. The NSA aren't going to pay us a visit. This software is eight years old. That's ancient, by NSA standards. My friend had to search the archives to even find a copy."

"First of all, I wasn't worried. Second, if I knew you couldn't handle it yourself, I could have given you a couple of people to call at the DEA who could have hooked you up."

"Thanks, but I have my own connections. And for your information, I could have handled breaking Harriman's files just fine. It might have taken longer, but I would have gotten it done."

"You have a website," I said. It came as no surprise Renita had a website. What did startle me was that, after all of the years we'd known each other, she'd never once mentioned it.

"Several."

"What sort of websites do you have, Renita?"

"There are some things about me you don't need to know...yet."

"Ain't that the truth," I said, trying to goad Renita into telling me about her websites.

Renita ignored my weak attempt. "Back to the business at hand," she said. "I've transferred copies of the accessible files to your PC. I've just started reading through the same files on my laptop while the network breaks down the rest. So far I haven't come across anything that raised my eyebrows."

"What about the message Harriman sent me? Was there any breakthrough on that?"

"I've been so focused on the files that I haven't given the message much thought. What I can tell you is this: that text message wasn't an offsite password to log on to his condo PC, or anything on or accessed by his PC."

I leaned back in my chair. The pieces were falling into place. "Let me throw a little something at you, Renita, to see what you make of it. Seven things happened near the time of Don Harriman's death. One, Harriman deliberately destroyed his laptop to prevent whoever was after him from getting vital information. Two, Harriman was able to send me an important clue before his assailants got to him. Three, Harriman was beaten in an effort to extract from him whatever information he had uncovered about something criminal. Four, Suzanne Kwong stumbled upon the near murder attempt, temporarily disrupting their plans. Five, Harriman was abducted. Six, Harriman was tortured. Seven, Harriman was murdered. By all indications, a professional operation. All in all, what do those series of events tell you?"

"The obvious. Harriman was onto something big enough to get him killed."

"Look beyond that; what else?"

Renita thought for a minute. "You've got me, C. J.," she said with a shrug of her shoulders.

"The manner in which things went down," I said. "Not only was the hit professional; the whole setup was. Whoever pulled the strings knew exactly what they were doing."

"Like a strong-arm protection racket."

"More like a security agency for large businesses."

"What sorts of people do business like that?" No sooner had Renita finished her sentence than her face lit with recognition. "An illegal one."

"You've got it. Harriman had uncovered something huge, and we need to expose what it is. When that happens, the rest will fall into place."

"Illegal narcotics?" Renita said.

"More than likely."

"Where, and who?"

"Let's not speculate too far beyond the facts. It could distort our necessity to keep an open mind. I have a couple of guesses, but nothing concrete."

"Any clues in the diary?" Renita asked.

"I now believe the whole diary is laced with clues. We just need the keys to unlock them." I paused for a moment. "We may have company on this case."

"Besides the Portland Police?"

"We don't have to concern ourselves with the PPB. Destini's giving us all the room we want. I think the DEA's keeping an eye on things."

Renita whistled. "Rolling with the big dogs."

"Right now the only rolling we'll be doing is through those computer files."

"Right," Renita said with a nod. We got to work.

CHAPTER FORTY-NINE

Renita and I worked late, pouring over what amounted to the legacy of Don Harriman's ongoing investigation. We read and repeatedly re-read, organized, categorized and labeled all of the pertinent information Harriman had on his condo PC. Having wrung the Don Harriman a.k.a. Barrette Wells angle dry, we elected to get a fresh start the following morning.

Amongst the items that appeared on Harriman's computer was a full list of Blue Sun properties. Beside some of the properties was an asterisk. It referred to a footnote that read, "Possible sightings, need more information." One of the properties earmarked with an asterisk was the torched rental property of Derek Knopp. Another of the properties was the former residence of Lisa and George Rundle, the people Destini had busted for the murder of their only child.

I contacted Destini about the possibility of interviewing the Rundles. Destini informed me I was too late. Both were dead. They had managed to hang themselves in their cells shortly after their convictions. After Destini mentioned it, I remembered reading about their suicides in the newspaper. No one could figure out how the leather belts the Rundles used to hang themselves with were smuggled into their cells. The suicides occurred on the same day. That was highly unusual, too. Typically, in a rock-bottom circumstance like the Rundles, one party would off themselves. Then, after the other party received the dire news, the other would try to follow suit. Both suicides were regarded as suspicious, but there was no hard evidence to prove anything. I asked Destini whether the Rundles were drug addicts.

"How'd you know?" Destini said in response to my question.

"I didn't, that's why I asked."

"Both turned out to be crackheads and heroin users. They never admitted it, but I believe their addiction drove them to murder their son for the insurance money. I still kick myself for not spotting the junkie angle sooner."

"Did you find any evidence they might have been manufacturing narcotics in their home?"

"To be honest, we never looked."

"Was either of them a chemist?"

"The mom kind of was. She minored in chemistry in college."

"Did they have any product on them when you busted them?"

"A few grams of heroin; only enough to keep them high for a couple of days. What's going on, C. J.?"

"It'll all be in my next report. I've got to go. Thanks, and I love you."

"Yeah, yeah, whatever. I love you, too." Destini said the last part quickly, then hung up. I would have laughed if I weren't so preoccupied with the Harriman case.

The former homes of Derek Knopp and Lisa and George Rundle were long shots worth pursuing. Harriman had mentioned in his files that the Knopp house had undocumented—and as far as he could tell, unauthorized—extensive modifications done from the original construction. Harriman went on to state what those changes were. His description corresponded with the same undocumented alterations that the Fire Marshall had found. I decided to follow in Harriman's footsteps. I returned to the scene of the Knopp fire, only to discover a new cookie cutter home in place of the charred rubble I needed to sift through for clues. A new resident had not yet moved in. I did what any good investigator would have done. I had a look around. The back door was locked. I picked it and went inside.

The house had been restored per the original plans. There were no signs of the modifications that existed before the house burned down.

I then made a trip to the former residence of the drug-addicted child killers. A nice young couple was renting the place. I misrepresented myself as an energy inspector for the electric company come to do a quick visual check for ways the couple might improve the energy efficiency of their home. They were all for it. Improved energy efficiency meant lower electric bills. Their residence was the same cookie cutter home as the new Knopp place. If it had been modified at some prior date, it didn't show. I expected as much. The people I was up against were organized and methodical. I would need to be agile to catch them.

I returned to my office to skim the diary. Confirmation was there. Everything had to be precisely laid out in order to get the help I needed. I spent the remainder of the day, and part of the night, mapping out a plan of attack.

CHAPTER FIFTY

I needed to walk on eggshells in order to put together a case that followed in Harriman's footsteps. Any request for information on the asterisked Blue Sun homes would send up a red flag to the people involved, if it wasn't already too late. We were dealing with a large scale, well-organized operation; one that could swiftly shut down and shift resources. The houses were spread out all over the northwest. I had to formulate a way to cobra strike at all locations. There was only one local person I knew that I could turn to for that kind of manpower.

Convincing Patrick O'Malley my plan would work was easy. He knew me well enough to realize I wouldn't ask him to take on such risks without having worked out the details beforehand. Patrick had the unenviable task of organizing a multi-state, multi-jurisdictional strike force. What I had in mind required more manpower than the Portland DEA Director had access to. He needed to enlist the Regional Director of the DEA and the FBI. Patrick also needed their aid in persuading a variety of judges to issue search warrants on what amounted to circumstantial evidence. Patrick called in every favor he had on the books in order to acquire the workforce he needed.

The whole thing went down like this: Patrick O'Malley took the information I brought him and persuaded a handful of trustworthy judges to sign search warrants for all of the residents that Harriman had asterisked, minus the former Knopp and Rundle residents. Patrick's raiding parties were already in position by the time the warrants were issued. They swooped in. They uncovered what we believed they would, in each case.

Those asterisked Blue Sun properties had been modified into laboratories for the production of illegal narcotics. At the same time, warrants had been issued for the seizure of all Blue Sun blueprints and city, state, and county construction documents that pertained to those same homes. Those documents proved that a number of homes had unauthorized laboratory installations. That meant under-the-table money was being paid to a number of people. The cobra strike worked to perfection.

It took time to sift through all of the evidence. Numerous arrests were made on a variety of charges ranging from bribery to first-degree murder. What became known as the Northwest Drug Cartel reached its tentacles into state, county and city government offices, building contractors, drug manufacturers and law enforcement. It was the largest bust of a domestic drug ring in the history of the Pacific Northwest.

The two men arrested for the murder of Don Harriman were blue-eyed Lenny Downs and brown-eyed Brian Kephart, the construction foreman and his assistant who had me fooled with their phony alibis. Much to Destini's chagrin, the foreman and his assistant were turned over to the FBI for agreeing to turn state's evidence on a number of Northwest Cartel sanctioned executions. Al and Tadpole also tried to cut a deal. Being low-rent collection men for the NW Cartel, they had little to offer. They were turned down.

New arrests were made almost daily. Authorities worked their way up the ladder. Janice Bigelow was charged for her part in the distribution of illegal substances through the U.S. Postal system. John Ullock was charged with knowingly supplying controlled substances for use in the manufacturing of illegal narcotics. And then there was Alice Baker.

CHAPTER FIFTY-ONE

Destini called me on my smartphone while listening to Smoky and Winston give a masterful evening jazz performance in Pioneer Square. The time had come for me to do my duty. Destini told me where I could find my perp.

Before presenting my cobra strike plan to the authorities, I came to an agreement with both Destini and Patrick (vis-à-vis the PPB, FBI, and DEA) to allow me to bring in Alice Baker. As a person of interest in an ongoing investigation, Ms. Baker had been warned by local authorities not to leave the area until the Blue Sun investigation had been completed. Both the FBI and DEA had round-the-clock surveillance on her to make certain she obeyed.

Alice Baker was sitting imperiously behind her desk when I arrived at her penthouse office. There was no one else in the penthouse. I was unarmed. I questioned the sanity of my decision. Ms. Baker had an expression that could kill. She was a person who had killed, according to the testimonies of Brain Kephart and Lenny Downs; although never by her own hand. Alice Baker was the Don of illegal narcotics manufacturing in the northwest. And no one could figure out why.

I approached Alice Baker with caution. She stood. Alice wore a Vera Wang blue strapless satin gown. Her brunette hair was luxuriously layered around her face. Light touches of cosmetics and tasteful jewelry topped off her elegant look. Alice Baker appeared ready for an evening of fine dining and ballroom dancing, not incarceration.

"Mr. Cavanaugh. What a pleasure it is to see you again," Alice said as she stepped from around her large marble desk to greet me with her open hand extended. Her voice was upbeat. I shook her hand. Alice smiled. A smile I did not return. Alice Baker was a lovely woman. She was clearly a person of genuine style and grace; a true femme fatale.

"It's time," I said. Her smile dissolved like granulated sugar in hot liquid.

"I know," she said with all of the weight of current realization.

"Before we go, do you mind telling me—"

"How I became involved in this mess."

"Yes."

"You wouldn't happen to be wearing a wire, would you?"

"No."

"Are there any recording devices of any kind on your person?"

"No."

"I have your word that you're not in any way equipped to entrap me."

"You have my word."

Alice Baker studied me for a moment before speaking. "And none of what I say to you will be repeated outside of this room."

"Not a syllable. I'm simply curious."

"I trust you, Cavanaugh. If nothing else, you are a man of integrity. So how did a nice girl like me wind up in a mess like this? It was economics, Cavanaugh, plain and simple. When I wanted to start my own real estate and construction company, the only element I lacked was capital. None of the legitimate lending institutions would take a gamble on me. They all said I had potential, but didn't have enough experience or collateral to cover my bet. I suppose I could have started small and scrimped and saved and squirmed my way up. That was exactly what I'd intended. Then John Ullock came back into my life."

"Back?" I said, realizing that this was something I had clearly missed.

"Yes, back. We ran into each other in a coffee shop in Vancouver, Washington. I was in Vancouver, feeling disappointed once again for having been turned down by another bank for a startup loan. Lock had become a pharmaceutical supplier. He was in the area making his runs at the local hospitals.

"I hadn't seen Lock in years. Lock was my marijuana connection in college. He was making decent money as a pharmaceutical supplier, but he said the big money was in the illegal stuff. He was raking in 20 times as much doing that. Lock was looking for businesses to legitimize his illegal profits. He agreed to front me the money I needed to get Blue Sun off the ground if I agreed to launder his seedy earnings."

"That's what friends are for," I said sarcastically.

"Hardly," Alice said, not playing along. "That was the only connection between Blue Sun and drugs, in the beginning. Then I got the idea. Lock's operation was only a few independent drug labs scattered over the northwest—what if we combined my construction and real estate business with his narcotics enterprise? We could net a fortune. I could work the underground capital into legitimate deals to expand Blue Sun. Lock agreed. And so it went.

"Our narcotics business grew so rapidly that we were having a distribution problem. We were forced to use too many mules. That left us open for ripoffs or employees becoming infatuated with our products; not to mention the very real possibility of exposure."

"Was drug addiction why the Rundles did what they did?"

"Yes; they became addicted, but not to our products. We deal strictly in synthetic designer drugs. Those idiots became hooked on crack and heroin. Lisa Rundle was one of our chemists. George became addicted to crack first. He dragged Lisa down with him. Somewhere along the line, they both added heroin to their nasty habits. We fired them once we discovered they had become junkies. There was no way anyone could have figured they would murder their own child in order to finance their addictions. That was a tragedy I never saw coming."

Alice looked away from me. She appeared to be staring into some great cosmic world from where the souls of all she had wronged were staring back in accusation. That solemn mood only lasted a half-minute before she righted herself. Alice began walking toward the large picture window on the west side of her penthouse office. I walked beside her. We stopped part way.

"We needed tighter control over distribution," Alice continued. "As fate would have it, Janice Bigelow walked into one of my real estate offices while I was meeting with the manager. Janice had answered an ad for an apartment at one of our rental properties. I hadn't seen Jan since college. We were both on the UDUB track team. Jan was also one of Lock's pot smokers. I took her to lunch to catch up on old times."

Janice Bigelow was another early connection I had missed. I had been so focused on Alice Baker and Don Harriman that everyone else had become secondary players in this drama.

"Jan was trying to get her health products mail order business off the ground," Alice continued. "She was strapped for startup capital, like so many entrepreneurs. I offered to help. All I asked in return was for Jan to handle all of our shipping needs through her company. Jan agreed. That allowed us to centralize our product distribution. All orders were prepaid, which minimized our risks. Once the shipment was accepted, all other matters were out of our hands. Jan never officially knew what we were distributing. She never asked. I never told her."

"Did Janice Bigelow or John Ullock have anything to do with your husband's death?"

"It wasn't intended for them to; but indirectly, yes. His diary was what we were after. We had tapped every other possibility of where Don would be compiling information on our operation—or so we thought. I didn't find out about his little hideaway until it was too late. Lenny Downs and Brian Kephart were supposed to execute Don in our home. But then that housekeeper showed up, and Jan and Lock had to intervene. They bought some time while Lenny and Brian took Don to Lock's place."

"Via the path in your backyard."

"Yes."

"That was quite a coincidence, the three of you being neighbors with connecting paths."

"There was nothing coincidental about it, Cavanaugh. Back when Lock and I consolidated, he lived in Renton, Washington. I suggested it would be better for business if we were in closer proximity to each other, as a matter of convenience. It would allow us more face time and less reliance on communication platforms that could be intercepted or monitored. Don and I had purchased a home in Crystal Gardens; a quiet, unassuming, upscale community, as you are well aware."

I nodded. She continued.

"A place that I believed would be perfect for our headquarters. Lock agreed. One of our next door neighbors, The Millers, were looking to sell their house and move to Florida. Lock made them an offer one and a half times their asking price. Of course, they couldn't refuse."

"Of course."

"A similar situation occurred with Jan. I had initially moved Jan into one of our Beaverton condos. The Allens, who lived on our other side, were anxious to unload their Crystal Springs home and move into their recently-completed Colorado mansion—that Blue Sun built, I'm proud to say. I bought their Crystal Springs home as a Blue Sun investment, and leased it to Jan.

"Living close did not necessarily mean privacy. Everyone in our neighborhood knew we were old college buds. We got the word out through the grapevine to make certain that they did."

That grapevine must have died by the time I got around to interviewing your neighbors, I thought, *because no one mentioned that fact to me.*

"Still, that might not explain to any neighborhood busybodies," Alice continued, "why a person in construction and real estate, a pharmaceutical supplier, and a health products guru would be spending so much time together. People talk and rumors fly—that's human nature. Plant the wrong bug in the wrong ear, and the next thing you know, someone from law enforcement is knocking on your door. We required a way to conduct face-to-face company business without the neighbors becoming curious. I had the paths constructed with that in mind. It gave us the private access we needed."

"Brilliant."

"I thought so."

"Back to Don, if you don't mind?" I said.

"Not at all. Now, where was I…ah, yes. Once the coast was clear, I had Lenny and Brian take Don to an out-of-the-way place and make one last effort at getting Don to tell us where his diary was."

I nodded.

"By the way, Cavanaugh, I did manage to get my hands on a copy of Don's diary—after the fact."

"How?"

"I have my sources."

That leak was probably someone inside the Portland Police Bureau.

I couldn't imagine how heartbreaking it must have been for Alice to sift through the sordid details of her husbands' infidelities in search of clues for what he knew about her operations. At the very least, her feelings had to blur her objectivity.

"I have to give you credit. I wasn't able to piece it together from Don's diary in the way that you did."

"I had more to go on than his diary."

Alice nodded. "The PC found in Don's hideaway. We totally missed your connection to that. We assumed the police had found it. We underestimated you, Cavanaugh."

"That happens a lot."

"We should have kept a closer eye on you."

"Lucky for me, you didn't."

"Lucky indeed."

"Regardless of whether your husband would have told them the whereabouts of his diary, in the end, your intent was to kill him."

Alice nodded.

"Did you know about your husband's infidelities?"

"Yes. The truth be told, I didn't much care." Alice looked at me for a moment. "I know what you're thinking. What a cold-hearted bitch I am."

"That's not at all what I'm thinking,"

"What are you thinking?"

"How difficult it must have been for you to kill the man you loved."

"If that damn maid hadn't shown up when she did," Alice said, avoiding my statement, "you and I wouldn't be having this conversation."

"If that maid hadn't shown up, and your plan went ahead as intended, would you have been able to stay in that house?"

Alice thought for a long moment. "Good point."

"You didn't dare harm Suzanne Kwong for fear it might draw a closer look at you."

"True. Not to mention, you and the maid had gotten rather chummy."

"But something changed your mind. Your boys trashed her place when they were looking for Suzanne."

"You're wrong about that, Cavanaugh; nothing changed. I sent Al and Tadpole to the maid's place to see if they could find the diary, and that was all. Fortunately for her, she didn't walk in on those two lugheads. Had she surprised those idiots, no telling what they would have done. Little did I know, the police already had the diary. Smart move, Cavanaugh, keeping that quiet; it kept us taking chances we wouldn't have normally taken."

"As you were saying," I said. I wanted to hear the whole story before Alice Baker changed her mind.

"Things were going great. Blue Sun was doing phenomenal. Jan and Lock were doing quite well with their legitimate businesses. By all accounts, we should have bagged the narcotics game and become 100% law-abiding. Funny thing about greed: it's rare you recognize it for what it is. Like junkies, we became addicted to the dirty money. I kidded myself into believing I went into business for the sake of building something. It was all about the bottom line at the end of the day.

"Derek Knopp put in a call to our Special Services Division of Blue Sun for an emergency plumbing problem. A plumbing problem meant that Knopp needed additional equipment. We were having Knopp shift from one product to another. We often did that with our chemists. It kept them from getting bored at doing the same thing time after time. Boredom can make you sloppy; mixing it up kept their level of concentration high.

"SSD were understaffed on that particular day due to vacations, a couple of people out sick, and an inordinate amount of orders. In case you haven't figured it out, Cavanaugh, SSD was the branch of Blue Sun that handled a wide variety of our druggists' needs."

I nodded. Alice continued.

"Don happened to be in the SSD office when the Knopp call came in. I still don't know what Don was doing there. Don decided to assess the Knopp situation for himself. That way he could determine whether it required bringing in a plumbing service. We informed Knopp that Don was on his way. Knopp took appropriate action. He packed up all chemical evidence and left the premises. That didn't stop Don. He let himself in with a passkey.

"It was around that time Don started sticking his nose in places where it didn't belong. Don told me about what he saw. He was convinced Knopp was using his self-made lab to make illegal narcotics. I tried to assuage Don. I explained to him that Knopp was a chemist who was probably messing around with some mad scientist crap. But Don wouldn't stop. He started investigating Derek Knopp and the modifications made on the house."

"Is that when you decided to get rid of Knopp?"

"You must understand something, Cavanaugh. Very few people knew I was involved in the Northwest Drug Cartel. I delegated what I wanted done through a Cartel Board of Directors. I'll bet if you asked the majority of people involved in the cartel who they thought was the mastermind behind it all, they would have said my husband. Few would have pointed a finger at me. It's a sexist attitude that persists. I was grateful. I used that ignorance to my advantage."

"You still haven't answered my question."

"I issued the orders to dispose of Knopp and have his property torched. Knopp was losing his cool. The closer Don got, the more rattled Knopp became. Knopp's product was primarily the club drug Ecstasy, at the time. He was also producing and selling a couple of other designer drugs on the side that he didn't think we knew about—an indiscretion that he had been warned would have serious consequences. I thought torching the house with Knopp in it was a good way to quell Don's curiosity. It would also serve as an example for the other chemist not to cross Blue Sun. Knopp was all for it. He thought we were going to burn down the house and set him up elsewhere. He even helped spread the gasoline. Imagine his surprise when he flamed up with the house."

I took a close look at Alice Baker. She had flippantly spoken those words. Her face and eyes told a different story. They told me she was agonizing inside over that resolution.

"When did you decide to murder your husband?"

Ms. Baker grimaced. Her stare hardened. She raised her head to the full length of her swan-like neck.

"When Don stopped telling me about his suspicions. You see, I knew Don was snooping around. He had gotten it into his head to check out every cookie cutter home that was similar to Knopp's. By chance, he wound up paying a visit to a number of my druggists. Each time he did, we were able to stay one step ahead of him. We got a SSD site cleanup team in, ahead of Don. Since most of our chemists worked legitimate jobs, doing what they did for us on the side, it was easy to arm them with cover stories in case Don grilled them about their activities. Don had little choice but to accept their explanations even if he didn't believe them. In any case, if my husband had confirmed the homes he suspected of containing drug labs were connected to Blue Sun, he'd have everything to lose, as well."

"Did you tell him that?"

"I told him nothing. What I hoped was that he would let it go."

"I suppose he wasn't as greedy as you."

"It wasn't only about money!" Alice shouted. Ms. Baker took a moment to calm herself. "It was about Blue Sun. I built this company. And nobody— I mean *nobody*—was going to take it from me; especially not some oversexed playboy who came along for the ride. Yes, I had him killed to protect my interest. Am I sorry? *Hell no.* Did I love him? Yes. Did I need him? No."

"You didn't know he was ex-FBI, I take it."

"He wouldn't have gotten close to me if I had known, love or not."

"Ain't love grand."

"Tell me something, Cavanaugh," Alice said without missing a beat. "Did Detective Pendleton suspect me in the murder of my husband?"

"You were at the top of her list, Ms. Baker."

"Infidelity on his part being my primary motive."

"That's what we initially suspected."

"Maybe, at the heart of it all, that was the real reason I had Don killed. I believed I had become numb to his womanizing. The truth could be that I loathed him for it."

"Why didn't you just leave him?"

"Had we divorced, it would have cost a lot to sever him from Blue Sun. Not to mention the full disclosure a financial probing of the company would have received in order to decide on fair equity for a divorce. It was too late, anyway. Don had already discovered too much. Sooner or later, it had to be done."

"Too bad for you it wasn't sooner."

"Too bad for me Don happened at all."

On the one hand, I couldn't pity Alice Baker. She was responsible for the production and distribution of illegal narcotics. My feelings ran the same for the person directly responsible for the mandated murders of a number of people. I did feel sympathy for the woman who had loved and lost. Compassion was not an emotion I would allow to surface.

"Why didn't you come after me or my partner?"

I believed I already knew the answer. Hearing the reasons from Ms. Baker would prove interesting.

"That was Lock's idea. I'll tell you what I told him: 'Are you nuts? We should go gunning for an ex-DEA agent—still in good standing with his former employer—who is romantically involved with one of PPB's finest homicide detectives?' That would have shined a spotlight on us for certain, and that was the last thing we needed. We operated best in the dark."

I nodded my understanding.

"Your partner, on the other hand, was a momentary consideration until we realized how close you two were. Although I'm not at all certain Detective Pendleton would have shed any tears over your partner's passing."

"Sounds as though you did your homework."

"You researched me. I researched you."

We walked up to the picture window. We stared out at the bright orange sun setting behind the smooth green surface of the Willamette River. The skyline cut sharp against the powdery blue sky. From the penthouse, the world seemed an innocent place. It was easier to ignore the parts that made up the whole. Individuals became insignificant; their only importance being how they wove into the tapestry of serenity we were observing from on high. A peaceful resonance pulsed from the whole picture postcard scene. It was a moment of unity between the trinity of human essence in harmony with nature. We were witnessing life at its best.

"I really loved Don," Alice said, a calm sense of acceptance melted into her voice.

"I know."

"I always did have terrible taste in men."

Her hands were clasped behind her back. Her chest out, shoulders erect and straight, poised, with confidence still radiating from her brown eyes, she stared out at the world as a queen surveying her domain.

"I suppose a bribe is out of the question," Alice said with a wry smile.

"It is. Even if it wasn't before, it's certainly too late now."

"True." Again, there was silence. "What do we do now?"

"Time to go, Ms. Baker," I said, absent of malice.

"It is a magnificent view from up here, isn't it?"

"That it is, Ms. Baker. That it is." There was a brief pause. "If it's any consolation, your husband refused to accept that you were behind any wrongdoing until the very end."

"What makes you so certain?"

"He constantly made excuses for you in his electronic journal regarding what he called the 'Blue Sun pipeline'. He never wanted to face the fact that you were behind it all. He loved you that much, in his own warped way."

Alice shuddered as if an arctic wind had swept through the office. "I knew what kind of man Don was before I married him," she said. "The same type of man I always seem to attract; the type who are never satisfied with one woman. Don was discreet in his affairs, and I chose to look the other way. When I needed or wanted him, Don was always there. He was a good lover and partner, an occasional confidant, and a friend. And yes, it was the most difficult decision of my life to order him killed. Don left me no choice. It was only a matter of time before he would have figured it out and turned me in."

"That's what you believe."

"About him figuring it out?"

"That he would have turned you in."

"It's what I know. Aside from him not being able to keep his dick in his pants, Don was a straight shooter. He wouldn't stand to be a party to anything or anyone that smelled illegal."

There was a pregnant pause. The blue of the sky had deepened. A few stars twinkled in the east. Content places for content beings.

"You do realize that just because you played the role of my confessor doesn't mean that anything I said to you will be repeated. I will deny everything when the time comes."

Alice Baker had not lost her edge. She was already calculating how to manipulate a lesser sentence, or maybe even an acquittal.

"I'd expect as much."

"What do you think my chances are, Cavanaugh?"

"That's not for me to decide."

"With all of the arrests, incriminating testimonies, and physical and circumstantial evidence the authorities have on the so-called Northwest Drug Cartel, they still don't have the complete story. Only I can give them that. I am the only one who knows everything. The names, places, quantities, shipments, financial records, front businesses, dates, and so on of the entire operation. That will be one of my bargaining chips. To give them the whole shooting match on a silver platter. Think it'll work?"

I gave Alice a deft nod. *Not if Destini or Patrick had anything to say about it*, was what I was thinking. Not to mention the people who had already been arrested and talked. There was probably more back room deal-making going on than at a used car lot.

"I'll bet my team of attorneys will be able to net me some sort of deal, especially if I agree to turn state's evidence against my associates."

"Honor among thieves."

"Honor is dead; buried alive by unabashed capitalism."

"Turning state's evidence may help your cause. Although there have been cases where those turned upon have exacted maximum revenge."

"Are you kidding?" Ms. Baker said with a grin. "I handled all of the rough stuff. My board wouldn't even know where to begin."

"I see." There was another pregnant pause. We stared at the setting sun. "Once again: it's time to go, Ms. Baker."

"C. J.—may I call you C. J.?" Alice said.

"If you'd like."

"Call me Alice."

I offered Alice my arm. She took it as a lady would. I shunned the awaiting police cruiser, allowing Alice one final walk of freedom.

We appeared to be enjoying a summer evening stroll together. There were double and triple takes along the way as a few people recognized the woman the newspapers had referred to as the suspected Don of the Northwest Drug Cartel. Alice graciously nodded and politely said, "Good evening" if someone stared for too long. Some scowled in response. Others responded in kind; albeit with a nervous edge.

Our conversation was lighthearted; almost genteel. There were no references made to her fate, the Northwest Drug Cartel, or the role I had played in her demise. I escorted Alicia Michelle Baker to the downtown Portland police station on a gorgeous summer evening, right into the cold pit of a maximum-security holding cell.

CHAPTER FIFTY-TWO

The discovery of the natural tunnels behind Alice Baker's home told me one thing. Destini and the uniformed officers who answered the Suzanne Kwong call did everything by the book. Had they taken the initiative and aggressively pursued Suzanne Kwong's account of what had happened, they might have been able to save Don Harriman. That was a tough call. With no physical evidence to support Ms. Kwong's account, they could not justify committing the manpower or man-hours. I elected to keep my musings to myself. Second and third guessing law enforcement is an easy thing to do. I wasn't there. That glaring realization earned investigating officers the benefit of the doubt, in my book.

In spite of all of her money and attorneys, Alice Baker wasn't fairing very well. The state turned down her offer to hand over everything she had on the Northwest Drug Cartel in return for a lighter sentence. The state also renounced her bid to turn state's evidence against her associates. As Alice had said, Blue Sun had an entire division dedicated to their operation. What she never expected was that the heart of her Cartel would ever be exposed. It was all on a data system cared for by an internet company called Sea Devil.

When Don Harriman began his investigation, he probably thought he would find a few houses that had been converted into drug labs. In all probability, he was convinced he was dealing with independent contractors. What he discovered must have shocked him: a large network of drug labs all over the Pacific Northwest. Their only common denominator was they were somehow connected to Blue Sun.

In all likelihood, it was around that time that he contacted Patrick O'Malley. Harriman was so certain he'd crack the case that he saw an opportunity to net himself a deal. One of the few things in life Harriman truly treasured was his FBI career. He had screwed that up. Fate offered him a reprieve. Maybe Harriman wanted back in the FBI. Or maybe he was just searching for a little redemption. He went for it, whatever his reasons. By the time Harriman deduced his wife was part of the NW Cartel, it was too late. The same could be said about the involvement of Janice Bigelow and John Ullock.

Harriman never located the data center. He did find the clandestine dark web site the Special Services Division used for their home base. All NW Cartel business was conducted through that site. You had to wade through eight internet links to log onto the server. Each link required a separate password. Failure to give the proper password at any link immediately truncated the connection. What Harriman had sent me was the first password needed to access the data center. The other seven, I'm guessing he didn't know or he would have probably turned that information over to Deputy Director O'Malley.

You had to give Harriman credit. His investigatory skills may have been rusty, but he managed to get the job done. Harriman was a good agent in spite of his trespasses. Maybe even good enough to get his FBI service record expunged.

Sea Devil was a front company buried deep in the Blue Sun books. Sea Devil was bankrolled exclusively by Blue Sun, who was their only real client. All other internet businesses Sea Devil had listed were phantoms. They didn't exist. On the Sea Devil system, authorities found everything pertaining to Blue Sun's Special Services Division.

The Feds and DEA backed out of their deal with Lenny Downs and Brian Kephart based upon those findings. They no longer needed their testimony. That meant the Portland Police could follow through on first-degree murder charges on Downs and Kephart. Destini was delighted. The Sea Devil discovery closed all legal loopholes. Alice Baker and everyone associated with the Northwest Drug Cartel were toast.

Renita and I had finished our paperwork on the Harriman case and were enjoying a celebratory glass of orange juice together in my office.

"I can see how everything fits together, except for the diary," Renita said.

"Harriman gave unique descriptions in his diary," I said. "Weird pet names for various sexual positions he experimented with during his adulterous rendezvous."

"So?"

"'We did the one and one deuce, double deuce dirty Powell. My pet description for this one is the 'one plus two with a double aught two Mill

Plain'. I like to call this one the 'double eight with an aught three Cornell twist.' Anything about those odd descriptions ring a bell?"

Renita thought for a minute before answering. "No."

"On the surface, it looks like twisted fun. But take into account the fact Harriman started in with those strange pet names and descriptions shortly after he began investigating the Northwest Drug Cartel."

Renita thought for half a minute, then shrugged her shoulders.

"Each of those odd references are street addresses on the Blue Sun property list. They also connect with each asterisked house in Harriman's PC files."

"When did you figure all this out?"

"Before I went to talk to Patrick about the cobra strike."

"Thanks for sharing."

"It was speculation, Renita. If I were 100 percent certain, I would've told you. You were still in the clear if it had blown up in my face."

"That's sweet, even if it is bull."

"I may not sleep with you, but that doesn't mean I don't care about you."

Renita didn't find what I said amusing. She looked irritated. "Save it, C. J.," she snapped.

"It was a huge gamble," I said, trying to step back into her good graces. "If I were wrong, we would be out in the middle of the ocean surrounded by legal barracudas. I saw no reason to risk both our careers. By keeping you out of it, I—at the very least—supplied you with a life raft to make it back to shore."

"Aren't you gallant?" Renita sarcastically said. "Sir Cavanaugh. In case you haven't noticed, I am a fully-grown, intelligent, resourceful, strong member of this investigation team. I believe I am capable of making my own decisions on what risks I should and should not take."

"If I was wrong and the Northwest Drug Cartel had been tipped off in time, or if I were erroneous in my guesses, those barracudas would have had my investigator's license. And don't think they would have stopped there. You would have been their next meal.

"Now, I respect how far you've come in this business, Renita. I would also be the first to note your valor and overall ability to handle yourself in a number of situations. But these people don't play. And rather than put you at unnecessary risk, I chose to take the plunge myself."

"I thought you'd learned by now." Renita slammed her empty glass on my desk. She rose and stomped toward the office door. At the doorway,

Renita turned to face me. One hand rested on her hip. She was wearing a loose-fitting, peach-colored sundress. Even that dress could not hide her taut athletic figure. I waited for her to speak. Her lips were pinched; her jaws set tight; her eyes narrowed and fierce. I had rarely seen Renita so angry. She slowly shook her head. Then, without warning, she turned and marched out of the office, slamming the door in her wake.

I was stunned. All I could think to do was add another installment to my encyclopedia of 'Why I'll Never Understand Women.' The telephone rang. I answered it.

"Congratulations!"

"Hey!" I almost said "kid", but stopped myself before the word hit my tongue. "Suzanne! How's it going?"

"Real well. I heard you got the bad guys—and gals."

"A whole lot of people got the bad guys and gals. Where are you?"

"Portland. I came to pack my things. I leave for New York next week, and I've got a ton of things to do. Thanks for taking care of my place. It looks better than when I lived here. You might have a second career in housekeeping."

"Renita and I took care of your place. She deserves half the credit. I'll pass along the career tip. She'll get as much of a kick out of it as I am."

"I'll bet. I appreciate what you did with my art."

"Have you visited the storage locker yet?"

"I took a peek." Suzanne's spirits dipped.

"Let us know if we can be of any help. We're here for you."

"Thank you," she said, rebounding. "You two have done more than enough already. What do I owe you?"

"Keep your nose clean and do your best in school and that should just about cover it."

"Deal," Suzanne said. We both laughed.

"Thanks for your help on this case," I said. "We couldn't have closed it without you."

"That was pure dumb luck; most of it bad."

"We would have never started the ball rolling in the right direction without your dumb luck.

"If you say so."

"How are your parents?"

"Great! I didn't realize how much I missed them. We had a chance to spend some quality time together. I was finally able to get through to them on what being an artist meant to me. My dad was the hard sell. He's kind of accepted it."

"Give him time. He'll come around."

"I'm doing it regardless," Suzanne said with her hardheaded stubbornness sounding through.

"Why do I get the impression you're a lot like your father?"

"I've heard that before," Suzanne said with a chuckle. "Before I leave for New York, mind if I drop by and do a sketch of you and Renita?"

"No problem. Stop by when you're ready. Renita may need to be warned. She'll need time to put on her face."

"I'll tell sis you said that."

"Oh, please don't, she'll kill me," I sarcastically said.

Suzanne laughed. "I'll tell her you said that, too. I've gotta go. I'll call before I drop by."

"That'll give me time to disappear."

"You'd better not!" Suzanne laughed. Her laughter faded into a moment of silence. I didn't know what to say. Suzanne had grown on me in much the same way as Renita. I was going to miss her.

"Thanks again," Suzanne said with a surprising sigh. I took that as a sign she was going to miss me as well.

"Just remember us when you're famous and rich."

"Like that's going to happen. I'm an artist, remember?"

"See you when I see you, Suzanne."

"Would tomorrow be too soon?"

"Tomorrow will be fine."

We hung up without saying goodbye.

CHAPTER FIFTY-THREE

Summer was drawing to a close. I needed fresh thyme and green beans for a special dinner I was preparing for Destini, Renita, Ernest, Suzanne and a few other friends at my place. I thought of taking the twins with me to the store, but they seemed content playing with each other in the back yard.

The walk to the corner grocer was uneventful. I noticed people, homes, trees, bushes and flowers, vehicles, movements, gestures, colors, textures, and the marquee statement that the market I was entering stocked over 100 different kinds of beers. It all seemed so mundane; so innocent.

Was something sinister always lurking beneath the brittle surface of our existence? Had the struggle from survival to dominance garnered such an evolution of lingering distress? Had we been reduced to predators stalking each other over demigod currency? Has currency become the go-between for our modern cannibalism?

I picked over the vegetables, found precisely what I needed, and added a twelve pack of Dentyne for Destini. Her favorite chewing gum was on sale.

"Have a nice day," the sales clerk said, "and try to stay dry." I accepted my change and looked outside. I had been so preoccupied with my thoughts, I hadn't noticed the light rain. I had come prepared. I thanked the sales clerk and stepped out into the rain.

A steady drizzle threatened to upgrade to a downpour. Rolling dark clouds supported that speculation. Warm drops of rain spattered my skin and hair. I unbound my umbrella and placed my thumb on the pushbutton release that would cause the umbrella to spring open. The rainwater felt refreshing: a natural shower; stimulating, yet soothing. I rebound my umbrella, using it as a walking cane for the remainder of my stroll home, bathing my soul in liquid sunshine. As for my smartphone—the verdict was still out.